the spring of candy apples

Other books in the Sweet Seasons series

The Summer of Cotton Candy

The Fall of Candy Corn

The Winter of Candy Canes

A Sweet Seasons Novel 

the spring of candy apples

debbie viguié

ZONDERVAN

The Spring of Candy Apples

This title is also available as a Zondervan ebook. Visit www.zondervan.com/ebooks.

This title is also available in a Zondervan audio edition. Visit www.zondervan.fm.

Requests for information should be addressed to:

Zondervan, *Grand Rapids, Michigan 49530*

Library of Congress Cataloging-in-Publication Data

Viguié, Debbie.
The spring of candy apples : a sweet seasons novel / by Debbie Viguié.
p. cm.
Summary: High school senior Candace struggles over decisions about college, boys, and friendship while working at the Candy Counter at The Zone amusement park.
ISBN 978-0-310-71753-9 (softcover : alk. paper)
[1. Amusement parks – Fiction. 2. Friendship – Fiction. 3. Interpersonal relations – Fiction. 4. Christian life – Fiction. 5. California – Fiction.] I. Title.
PZ7.V6727Sp 2009
[Fic] – dc22 2008042461

All Scripture quotations come from the King James Version of the Bible.

Published in association with the literary agency of Alive Communications, Inc., 7680 Goddard Street, Suite 200, Colorado Springs, Colorado 80920. www.alivecommunications.com

Interior design: Christine Orejuela-Winkelman

Printed in the United States of America

---

11 12 13 14 15 16 17 /DCI/ 23 22 21 20 19 18 17 16 15 14 13 12 11 10 9 8 7 6 5 4 3

To all the friends and family who have spent time with me in theme parks and listened while I talked about The Zone—thank you!!

Also, thank you to the wonderful group at Zonderkidz, especially Betsy Flikkema, who helped make these books a reality.

1

Candace wondered how every couple of months she managed to wind up seated across the desk from a Zone executive. Only this time it wasn't Lloyd Peterson, the hiring manager, it was John Hanson, owner of the theme park himself. Nor was this a small office among many in the building she had gotten almost used to visiting. This office was huge. Trophies from John Hanson's football days glistened from various alcoves around the room. His desk was the size of her bed at home. It was as though everything in the office had to be enlarged to fit his larger-than-life personality.

Just breathe, she reminded herself. She let out the air she had been holding in her lungs and tried very hard not to squirm in her seat. He was smiling and friendly, but there was so much more at stake this time than a part-time, seasonal job.

"So, Candace, as one of the five finalists for The Zone GameMaster scholarship, you must be pretty excited," he said.

Excited. Bewildered. Nervous. So many to choose from. Excited because the winner got a full scholarship to a college in Florida. Bewildered because she still couldn't believe her Balloon Races doodle could be taken seriously as a potential ride by anyone. Nervous because she didn't want to blow it.

With a start, Candace realized that she had been staring into space. "Yes, I'm very excited ... and pretty nervous," she stammered.

"Just try to relax," he urged.

"I'll try."

"Now, as you know, there are many stages in the competition, and you've passed them all to get this far. During the first stage, contestants who don't meet the qualifications are weeded out. Next, the Game Masters take a look at the attraction concepts for viability. Then they announce the top twenty candidates."

Candace remembered how shocked she had been at that announcement. She didn't even know she was a contestant. Over the summer, she doodled her Balloon Races idea on a napkin. She had been about to throw it away but gave it to Josh instead, and he had secretly entered it in the scholarship competition. Now it was nearly March and she was a finalist. She was upset at Josh at first, but if she won, she'd have to get him an awesome thank-you present.

"At that point," continued Mr. Hanson, "we announce the candidates and give everyone who works for The Zone a chance to submit a recommendation for a candidate. Now, this isn't some sort of popularity vote. A recommendation is a serious thing. The person filling it out has to take the time to submit a ten-page form evaluating the candidate's strengths and telling the search committee exactly why they believe that person should have the position. Based on the strength and numbers of those recommendations, the group of twenty is narrowed to five."

"Wow! I can't believe enough people took the time to recommend me," Candace said.

"Several people here think quite highly of you. You had enough recommendations to just beat out a young gentleman for the fifth spot."

"So, I'm here because I had one more recommendation?"

"Essentially, yes. It's policy that we don't allow contestants to see their recommendations. However, since you are in the top five, I can tell you the people who recommended you."

Candace suddenly realized her heart was in her throat. This somehow made her more nervous than the interview itself. It was a reflection of what people thought of her and how they had chosen to support her. She found herself holding her breath again as she waited for the names.

"You had nine recommendations. You received recommendations from your supervisor, Martha; Kowabunga referee Josh; Muffin Mansion's Becca and Gib; Sue from janitorial; Roger from the Dug Out; and Pete, the train operator."

None of those came as a great surprise, but Candace was touched and flattered that they all spent the time and effort on her. She made a mental note to thank them all later.

"You received the eighth one from Rose in the nurse's office."

Candace smiled. It seemed like every few months she ended up there after some kind of catastrophe. It was nice to know she had managed to make some kind of positive impression. That had to mean the final recommendation that had put her over the top was from her boyfriend, Kurt. She felt a warm glow as she thought about the special thank-you kiss she'd have to give him.

"And the last one was from Lisa in food carts."

Candace sat stunned for a minute. It wasn't Kurt, but Lisa, the girl who hated her? "Are you sure about that?" she burst out.

John looked surprised. "Yes. Why?"

"Nothing," Candace mumbled, dropping her eyes.

The owner of the park chuckled. "Sometimes it's a surprise when we discover who notices us."

She nodded.

"And so, here you are, one of the final five contestants."

"What happens from here?" Candace asked.

"This is it. I stay out of the selection process until the very end. Now I interview the five candidates and choose the winner."

Candace had suspected that might be the case, but actually knowing made her start to sweat even more.

"You've been doing seasonal work for us, is that right?"

"Yes."

"You know, I think it's time to upgrade you. How would you like to work part-time at the Candy Counter?"

"In the Home Stretch?" she asked.

"That's the one."

"That would be great," she said, not sure what else to say at the moment. She hadn't really had a chance to think about working during the spring. There was a part of her that was instantly excited, though. Working at the Candy Counter meant she wouldn't be working at a food cart.

"So, shall we begin the interview?" he asked, the smile leaving his face.

She nodded mutely.

When Candace finally left the interview, she was shaking. She had done her best, but it had been very intimidating knowing that her answers could change a lot of things for her. Not quite ready to go home, she headed into the theme park to track down a couple of her friends.

The Zone was one of the biggest, coolest theme parks in Southern California. It was separated into several different areas, called zones, such as the Exploration Zone where she headed first. All the terminology of the park was geared toward sports and competition. Workers were called referees; costumed characters were called mascots; and customers were called players. *On field* referenced areas inside the park, while *off field* included the areas behind the scenes where players couldn't go. The goal of the park was to entertain, educate, and inspire healthy competition in every area of life.

Candace had visited the park often as a child, but she hadn't truly fallen in love with it until the summer before when she had gotten her first job working as a cotton candy operator. She had made a lot of good friends in the park, and as she approached the Muffin Mansion she couldn't help but smile at the thought of one of them in particular.

There were no customers inside the Muffin Mansion, and Candace made a beeline for Becca who was operating the cash register. Candace jumped up so she was sitting on the counter, leaned over, and gave Becca a big hug.

"What was that for?" Becca asked.

"For recommending me. I've got a hug for Gib too. Is he here?"

"He should be back from break in a minute."

"I'll wait."

"So, how did the interview go?" Becca asked.

"I'm not sure. I'm pretty nervous about it," Candace confessed.

"Everyone probably felt that way."

"I don't know. I'm still not even sure how I got this far in the competition."

"Are you kidding? Balloon Races looks awesome."

"How do you know?"

Becca smiled. "Josh has been showing a copy of your drawing to everyone."

Candace rolled her eyes. "Great. One more thing I've gotta kill him for."

"Hey, go easy on the guy. If you get that scholarship, you'll owe him big time for entering you."

"Yeah, I know," Candace admitted.

"What's wrong? You've got frowny face," Becca said.

"Kurt didn't recommend me for the competition," Candace admitted.

"Ouch," Becca said, wincing.

"And Lisa did. Isn't that weird?"

"Definitely freaky."

"My birthday is coming up in a couple of weeks," Candace said, changing the subject.

"Happy early birthday," Becca said.

"I'm thinking of having a slumber party a week from Friday, and I wanted to know if you would come."

"I'll be there!" Becca said.

"Cool."

"How many people are coming?"

"I'm not sure yet. You're the first one I've officially invited."

"Let me guess. You figured that it would be a party even if I was the only other person there?" Becca teased.

Candace laughed. "No sugar for you."

"You're cruel."

Kind was more like it. Becca had some sort of weird allergy that made her completely crazy hyper when she had sugar. Every few months she managed to get hold of some and cause complete chaos.

"How did yer interview go?" a deep voice suddenly asked.

Candace jumped off the counter and hugged a surprised Gib. He patted her back awkwardly.

"Thank you for nominating me," she said.

"It was no problem. Glad to do it."

"Tell the truth. Was it so you'd never have to worry about me slipping Becca some sugar?" Candace asked with a smile. Over the summer, Gib had explained Becca's sugar allergy to Candace and forbade her to give the other girl cotton candy.

Gib smiled. "I figger you and I are already clear on that matter. Nah. I nominated you because you show initiative and courage and have a way of shaking things up."

Candace gave him another hug and then pulled away laughing. "Well, thank you. I really appreciate it."

"Kurt didn't nominate her," Becca said.

"Knave!" Gib said, his face darkening.

Before Candace could respond, players came through the door. She gave Becca and Gib a little wave and headed out.

Once in the clear, she headed for the Splash Zone, hoping to catch Josh. She saw him in his tank top and shorts in front of the Kowabunga ride.

"You've gotta be cold," she said as she walked up.

"It's worth it to freeze now so I don't have to sweat through the summer," he said with his customary grin. "So, how'd it go?"

"I don't know," she confessed as she gave him a hug. "But thank you for nominating me. Thank you for *entering* me," she said, laughing a little.

"Told you the Balloon Races was cool," he said.

She stepped back with a laugh. "Remind me to listen to you more."

"That's an easy one."

"So, do you think I have a shot?" she asked.

He grew serious for a moment. "I hope so, but I don't know. I entered you and I nominated you. That was really all I could do. It's out of my hands."

"I know. I'm just nervous."

She was about to tell him who had nominated her when she remembered she had other news. "I did get a part-time job out of it," she said.

His eyes widened. "Seriously? Part-time, not seasonal?"

She nodded. "I'm going to be working at the Candy Counter."

"That's great! Congratulations. I'm going to miss seeing you on the carts, though."

She shrugged. "We can still hang on breaks."

"Absolutely. Well, that is, after Talent Show. My team and I are practicing a lot."

Candace blinked at him. "Talent Show? What Talent Show?"

Josh laughed. "Same old Candace."

Another referee walked up. He looked familiar to her, but Candace couldn't place him.

"Looks like I'm on break," Josh said. "Candace, have you met Mark yet?"

"We double-dated a few months back," Mark said, smiling at her.

Then Candace remembered who he was. Her best friend Tamara had gone out with him once on a pity date. He had seemed like a really nice guy, just not Tam's type.

"How have you been?" Candace asked.

"Good. Really good. Actually I should thank you."

"Why?" she asked.

"You and your boyfriend made working here sound like so much fun. That's why I applied to work here too."

"And you've been enjoying it?" she asked.

"Check."

Mark took over Josh's position, and then Candace walked away with Josh.

"I'm glad he's having fun," she said.

"Yeah, Checkmark's going to be okay."

"Checkmark?" she asked.

"Yup. That's what people have nicknamed him. If you ask him anything, he says 'check' instead of 'yes' or 'got it.' "

"Hence Checkmark."

"Check," Josh said with a grin.

"Okay, so what's this about a talent show?" Candace asked him. As usual she seemed to be one step behind as far as the information went.

"It's a big deal every year about a week after Easter. There's a party and talent competition for all the refs."

"What, like singing and dancing?"

Josh rolled his eyes. "Only if you're, like, amazing at one of those. Mostly groups try to come up with new stuff. The winners last year did a whole Chinese acrobat show. Of course, it helped that three of them were exchange students, brothers who were actually acrobats."

"Great, no pressure," Candace said. "When do sign-ups start?"

He laughed. "You mean, when do they finish, as in, this week."

"Oh, no," Candace groaned. Her experiences at The Zone had taught her that those who did not sign up early got stuck with teammates they did not pick. That very thing happened to her at the summer Scavenger Hunt. Luckily, though, her team had been awesome. Not only had they won, she had also made some great friends from the experience.

"I'm guessing you're already on a team," she said to Josh.

"Sorry," he said with a shrug. "Us Kowabunga guys kinda stick together. Besides, you said you weren't going to be working Easter."

She shrugged. "You know what they say. The more things change ..."

"The more they stay the same," Josh finished with a grin.

"It looks like it's time to get the team back together."

"Good luck with that."

"What talent do you Kowabunga guys have?" Candace asked.

"We have many. If you're referencing the contest, though, we're keeping that under wraps a little while longer."

"Come on, I can keep a secret," she said.

"I know you can," he said with a sly smile.

The truth was she had been keeping Josh's secret—a big one—for months. Her best friend, Tamara, had only recently found out what it was, but through no fault of hers.

"You wanna hear a secret?" Candace teased.

"Sure."

"I think my best friend's crazy about your brother."

"Well, that's a relief, since I know my brother is crazy about your best friend."

Crazy was an understatement. Tamara and James had met a couple of days before Christmas and had spent so much time together the last eight weeks, it seemed like one long date as opposed to dozens of short ones. Candace had seen more of

Josh socially in the last few weeks than she had in the preceding eight months. Somehow the two of them ended up at the movies or the theater or dinner with James and Tamara more often than not. She was seeing more of Josh than she was of Kurt.

She briefly thought about asking Kurt about the talent contest, but he was a mascot, and they usually did things as a group. She was going to have to hunt down some old friends.

"What's wrong with you?" Tamara asked an hour later as Candace plopped into the chair across from her at Big D's, their favorite ice-cream parlor.

"I gotta get the team back together," Candace said.

"Same question, let's try for a new answer," Tamara said.

Candace sighed. "Talent Show competition at The Zone after Easter. Not only do I have to get a team, but I've got to have a talent."

"Girl who doesn't work at the park, say 'what?'" Tamara asked.

"The beginning?" Candace asked.

"Yes, please. And don't leave anything out," Tamara cautioned.

Candace smiled. She and Tamara had been best friends forever. Sometimes it was like they could read each other's minds. Other times it was like they were communicating in completely different languages. It wasn't that far of a stretch. They practically came from different planets.

Tamara came from money, lots of it. Fortunately for Candace, all that money hadn't made Tamara a snob, just overly generous. Tamara was also one of those scary-beautiful people with long dark hair and olive skin. Candace, with her middle class upbringing, average good looks, and red curls came from a totally different background. The only things they shared were school, church, and a lifelong friendship and respect. Their friendship had suffered when Candace first started working, but that was all in the past. She was still sure, though, that Tamara wasn't going to be pleased that Candace had managed to tie up more weekends and spring break with The Zone.

"The interview went okay. I was nervous, but I didn't faint or anything like that," Candace started.

"And?"

"And he offered me a regular part-time job at the Candy Counter."

"In the Home Stretch?"

"That's the one."

"And you said yes?"

Candace nodded.

Tamara leaned back with a sigh. "There goes spring break."

"What about James?"

"He works too."

"Bummer."

"Tell me about it. I was counting on spending days with you while he was at work."

"Well, maybe I'll get night shifts," Candace said.

"We can only hope," Tamara said with a sigh.

Candace smiled. "VH?" she asked, meaning "Virtual Hug."

"VH."

2

Candace couldn't believe how nervous she felt as she headed for The Zone and her first shift at the Candy Counter. In some ways it was just as bad as getting her first job there. Unlike the other jobs she'd had at The Zone, this one didn't come with a built-in expiration date. She was there until she quit. *Or at least until they fire me*, she thought ruefully.

The uniform was similar to the one she had worn over the summer. She wore white shorts, white Keds, and a striped blouse. Instead of pink and white stripes, though, the blouse was striped with multiple colors representing the dominant color of each zone in the park. The Candy Counter was on the Home Stretch, the array of shops and restaurants at the front of the park that visitors had to traverse on their way in and on their way out.

She arrived at the park and made her way toward the store. She had just reached it when she spotted Josh, jogging toward her with a camera in hand.

"What are you doing?" she asked.

He grinned. "Just wanted to get a picture of Candy's first day at the Candy Counter."

She didn't want to, but she couldn't help smiling back at him. "Fine, but just one picture."

"Okay, now stand under the sign," he instructed.

She positioned herself under the *Candy* in the sign and struck a pose.

"Beautiful," he said as he took the picture.

He moved to show it to her on the screen. She laughed when she saw herself.

"Oh yeah, this is going to make a great addition to The Zone Yearbook," he said.

"What?" she asked, the laughter dying on her lips.

"The yearbook. Comes out at the end of May each year."

"You're kidding," she said.

"Nope."

"I've never heard of a Zone yearbook!"

"Candy, there are lots of things here you've never heard of. Still, you're going to be pretty popular in the book this year."

"Give me the camera."

"So you can delete the picture? I don't think so. Besides, isn't it time for your shift?" he asked.

"Fiend."

"That's friend," he corrected.

She rolled her eyes and stepped into the store.

"Surprise!"

Candace jumped backward as dozens of people shouted in unison. Behind her, Josh put a hand on her shoulder and pushed her forward.

Bewildered, she took in the scene. There were balloons everywhere, and a huge banner said Happy Birthday & Welcome Aboard! Everywhere she looked she saw familiar faces of friends and coworkers.

"What's going on?" she asked.

"Well, someone let slip that your birthday is coming up," Martha, one of Candace's supervisors, said. "And then you became a regular nonseasonal employee, and it just seemed like a good excuse to celebrate."

"You guys! Wow, thank you!" Candace exclaimed.

"So, I take it you didn't see the sign on the door that said Closed for Private Party?" Becca asked.

"Nope, she was too busy trying to get me to delete her picture," Josh said proudly.

She turned on him and pounded him in the chest with a fist. "You big faker. I knew there wasn't a yearbook!"

"Oh no, there's a yearbook," Pete, the crazy train engineer, spoke up. "I'm guessing you're going to be all over it this year."

"Great," Candace said with a shake of her head. "Okay, so who actually works here?" she asked.

Several hands shot up around the room, and soon Candace's newest coworkers were making their way forward to introduce themselves. Names and faces blurred by for a minute, and Candace realized that she wasn't going to remember them. Oh well, there'd be plenty of time to get to know everyone later, she decided.

Once the introductions were finished, a cake with candles was wheeled out. On top *Candy* was spelled out in a variety of different candies. She smiled, blew out the candles, and received the first piece. It was strawberry cake, and it was amazingly good.

"Who made this?" she asked.

"We did," Traci, one of her new coworkers, said. "We make special-occasion cakes here."

"I didn't know that," Candace admitted.

"It's a well-guarded secret," Martha explained. "If it got out how good the cakes were, they wouldn't have time to make anything else."

"I can believe it," Candace said. She made her way gradually around the store, trying to thank everyone. She finally found Roger.

"Happy almost birthday," he said.

"Thanks. How are you doing?"

"Pretty good. It looks like I'm going to get a sports scholarship to college."

"Roger, that's amazing!" It really was. When she had met Roger, he had been the clutziest guy in the park. Their team had won the summer Scavenger Hunt, though, and it gave Roger the confidence he needed.

"And thanks to your nomination, you might have gotten me a scholarship. That's very thoughtful of you," she added.

"Well, you know. Us Scavenger Hunt winners have to stick together."

"So, Roger, I hear there's a talent show coming up. How about getting the team back together?" she asked.

He squirmed slightly. "I'm sorry, Candace. That would be fun, but I'm trying to get a job at the Muffin Mansion. If I get it, I'll be on their team."

"Becca told me they almost never have openings."

"One of the ladies, Sally Lunn, is retiring."

"Wow, really?"

"Yeah. She's seventy. So that means there's going to be an opening, and I want to be the one to get it."

"So you can spend more time with Becca?"

He nodded.

"Good for you! I hope they pick you."

"Me too," he said.

Muffin Mansion referees did all the park activities together. It was a very close-knit group. They were fiercely competitive and completely loyal to each other.

"Hey, stranger," Sue said.

"Hey!" Candace said, giving Sue a quick hug.

The other girl worked in janitorial, and they'd been friends since the beginning of summer. At Christmas, Candace had discovered that a family tragedy had left Sue to raise her two younger siblings, and Candace and some of the others had done their best to help the family out.

"How are things going?" Candace asked.

"Really great," Sue said with a smile. "Remind me to thank you."

Candace waved her hand. "Thank you for coming to this."

"Hey, any chance at free cake and I'm there," Sue joked.

"And, seriously, thanks for nominating me, I really appreciate it."

Sue shrugged. "I can't think of anyone who deserves it more."

"I've been meaning to hunt you down. I'm having a slumber party for my birthday next Friday night. Do you think there's any way you could come?"

It was a long shot, given Sue's brother and sister, but it never hurt to ask.

"I'll see what I can do. A couple parents owe me some sleepover favors."

"That would so rock!"

"So, has anyone told you about Talent Show yet?" Sue asked.

"Just found out about it," Candace admitted. "Have you got a team yet?"

"Yeah, Pete, Traci, Corinne from food services, and I signed up last week."

"Oh," Candace said, unable to hide her dismay.

Sue smiled. "We put your name down too, just in case."

"Really?"

Sue nodded.

"You guys are the best," Candace said, hugging her again.

"Pete had a sneaking suspicion you'd be back. I knew if you were, you'd be the last to hear about Talent Show."

"Well, you were both right," Candace said. "So, what's our talent?"

"We have a meeting planned to discuss it. I'll email you the details."

"Cool, thanks."

Sue moved away to talk to someone else, and Candace continued to move through the store, hugging and thanking people. Finally, in a far corner, she found Kurt.

"Happy birthday," he said, giving her a kiss on the cheek.

"Well, almost," she said. "It's not for a few more days."

"Oh. We'll have to do something to celebrate," he said.

"I thought you'd never ask."

For a brief moment she considered asking him why he hadn't nominated her, but it didn't seem like the time or place to start that conversation.

After two hours, Martha declared the party officially over. Candace's first official job as a Candy Counter referee was cleaning up from her own party. It was funny, but she was glad to do it. By the time the place was spotless, her shift was over.

"Traci and Candace, you two can take off," the supervisor said.

Candace and Traci walked outside and ran straight into Lisa.

"Well, if it isn't the park princess," Lisa sneered.

Lisa was Kurt's ex-girlfriend. She'd had it in for Candace since the day they met. She had even tried to get Candace fired over the summer. They occasionally shared an uneasy truce, but this was clearly not going to be one of those days.

"Lisa, I'm not in the mood," Candace said, surprising herself by saying it out loud.

"Oh, forgive me, Princess. As a mere commoner, I'll get out of your way."

"Lisa, don't be like that," Candace started to say, but the other girl stalked off.

"Wow, she *really* doesn't like you," Traci noted.

"She thinks if I weren't around, she and Kurt would get back together," Candace explained.

"Somehow I don't think all of this is about a guy," Traci replied.

"Really?"

Traci nodded.

It was a strange thought. Could there actually be some other reason why Lisa didn't like her? Candace shoved the thought aside impatiently. She didn't want to think about Lisa.

When she reached the Locker Room and got her things out of her locker, she saw that she had a message from Tamara on her phone.

"Candace, I need you to come over after work. It's a total crisis," Tamara wailed.

Candace tried calling her back, but it went straight to voicemail. Candace left a brief message before heading for the parking lot. Ten minutes later she parked in front of Tamara's house.

"So, what's the crisis?" Candace asked as Tamara opened the door.

Tamara didn't say anything, but grabbed her by the hand and led her upstairs. A dozen dresses were draped across her bed and what had to be thirty pairs of shoes littered the floor.

"Did a bomb go off?" Candace joked.

Tamara sat down on the floor with a frustrated sigh, shoving shoes to the side.

The room had been in similar condition a couple of weeks earlier when Candace helped Tamara pick out what she was wearing for her Valentine's Day date with James. Kurt had been working that day, so Candace had all the time in the world to help Tamara out. She still wished she and Kurt could have done something fun and romantic, though.

"Seriously, what gives? I don't think I'm missing a holiday," Candace said.

"Today is our two-month anniversary of dating," Tamara explained.

"Ah. So where is James taking you?"

"I don't know. He wouldn't tell me," Tamara admitted.

"Did he give you an idea of what to wear?"

"No!"

"I see the problem. Give me one minute," Candace said. She stepped into the hall and pulled her cell phone out of her pocket. A moment later she heard Josh's voice.

"Candace?"

"Hey, yeah, it's me."

"How are you?"

"Good, but we need some wardrobe guidance over here."

"He hasn't told me where they're going."

"Can you find out?"

"Not likely."

Candace sighed. "Well, can you at least find out what he's wearing?"

"Hold on."

A minute later Josh was back. "Tux."

"Thanks, Josh."

"Don't thank me quite yet. James has a way of being unpredictable. He could just as easily change into jeans halfway through the date."

"Okay, how on earth do we plan for that one?"

"Unfortunately, you don't. Not really. Trust me, if it had been crucial that she wear something specific, he would have given her fair warning."

"Good to know," Candace said. "I gotta go."

"Later."

Candace walked back into Tamara's room. "He's wearing a tux."

Tamara's face lit up. "That will be so much easier," she said.

"Let's hope so," Candace muttered under her breath.

An hour later Tamara looked stunning in one of her favorite purple formals and matching pumps. Candace had helped her put her hair up.

"You know, this guy has really done something for you," Candace commented.

"How do you mean?"

"Somehow you're even more beautiful. Your eyes are always shining."

"It's called love," Tamara said with a contented sigh. "I highly recommend it."

Candace smiled. As much as she liked Kurt, she had never been sure she could actually say she was in love. Watching

Tamara with James, she was becoming more and more sure that she wasn't. She was also questioning her hypothesis that she and Kurt might be in love someday.

"What's wrong?" Tamara asked.

"Nothing," Candace said. There was no need to bring Tamara down with her love problems. At least not right before James arrived.

As if on cue, the doorbell downstairs rang.

"Can you get it?" Tamara begged.

"Want to make a grand entrance?"

"You know it."

Candace hurried downstairs and opened the front door. James was standing there in a tuxedo holding a bouquet of flowers. She was relieved to see that Josh's intel had been right on the money.

"Come in," Candace said.

"Thanks."

James stepped in the house, and Candace had to admit that he looked just as good in a tuxedo as Josh did. Where Josh brought a look of casual elegance, James brought an air of excitement and mystery.

"Can I get you a martini, Mr. Bond?" she teased.

"Shaken, not stirred," he said with a grin.

Tamara appeared at the top of the stairs, and Candace heard him suck in his breath sharply.

They did make a gorgeous couple. Candace was pretty sure that two months was a dating record for Tamara. Her friend had always had a string of guys dangling after her, but since she had met James, she seemed to have eyes only for him. Candace stepped into the living room for a moment to give them some space.

Her phone rang.

"Hello?"

"Hey, it's Kurt. Do you want to grab some dinner?"

"Sure, where?"

"IHOP."

"So breakfast it is," she quipped.

"Meet me there in thirty."

"Okay."

She hung up the phone and moved back into the foyer.

Tamara had already managed to put her flowers in water and was ready to go. Candace wondered wistfully where James was taking her. Knowing him, it could be somewhere really nice or somewhere really fun.

"So, where are you guys going?" she asked.

James smiled. "Can't ruin the surprise."

Candace nodded. Wherever it was, she bet it wasn't IHOP.

3

"My sister is getting married," Kurt said by way of greeting.

"Congratulations," Candace said as she slid into the booth across from him.

Candace couldn't remember him ever talking about a sister. Then again, Kurt didn't spend much time talking about his family at all.

"When?" she asked, after a long pause in which he didn't seem ready to say anything else.

"Easter weekend."

"Interesting choice."

"Yeah."

"Do you know the guy very well?"

"They've been dating for a while," Kurt said with a shrug.

"How old is your sister now?"

"Twenty-one."

Only about three years older than Candace. She shivered for a moment. She couldn't imagine being ready to marry anybody in three years' time. *Then again, if I met Mr. Right, maybe that would change.*

For a moment, she sat very still as the impact of that thought came home to her. *Kurt's not Mr. Right.*

She had always known that, or at least, always suspected. She felt very, very sad, but also somehow relieved. She shook her head and returned her attention to Kurt. Fortunately, he seemed too lost in his own thoughts to notice that she had been lost in hers.

What should I do? she wondered. Kurt was her first boyfriend, and she still hadn't really gotten good at being a girlfriend. How on earth was she supposed to break up with him? Tamara would know. She thought about running to the bathroom and calling her, but remembered Tamara was on her date with James.

Tamara and James. In a way, watching the two of them had really helped Candace see that she and Kurt just didn't seem to fit together.

"What are you going to eat?" Kurt asked loudly enough to startle her.

"Ummm … I don't know," Candace said, flipping open the menu and trying to scan it with eyes that weren't even registering the words.

When the waitress came, Candace ordered pancakes with strawberries, not because she wanted it, but because it was the only thing she could remember having had there before.

"Are you okay?" Candace asked Kurt after the waitress had left. She was busy with her own freak-out, but at least she could tell that something was troubling him.

"Yeah. It's just hard to think of my sister as being old enough to get married."

"I get that," Candace said. "My mom was my age when my parents got married. Can you imagine?"

She was babbling, and she knew it. She screeched to a halt, hoping he wouldn't have any response.

"Yeah," he said instead.

She panicked. She and Kurt were discussing marriage. Well, not marriage between them, but marriage in general and it was scaring her. What if he thought everything was fine with them?

What if he really loved her and was thinking their relationship was long-term?

Candace stood up suddenly.

"What is it?" he asked.

For one dizzying moment she thought about telling him the truth. He deserved better than to be dumped in the middle of an IHOP, though. "I have to go to the bathroom," she said and then rushed off.

In the restroom, she splashed some cold water on her face with hands that shook. What on earth was she doing? She wanted nothing more than to be home in bed curled up with Mr. Huggles, her stuffed bear. Instead she was in a coffee-shop restroom, her heart was pounding, and she felt like she was going to be sick.

Date or no date, she needed to talk to Tamara. She pulled out her cell phone and called, but it went straight to voicemail. "What am I going to do?" she asked her reflection.

She called Josh.

"Hey, Candy, what's up?"

"Josh, I'm in the bathroom at IHOP. Kurt's at the table, and I don't want to go out there because I think I need to break up with him, and I don't know what to do and I'm freaking out."

"Whoa, slow down. First off, are you okay?"

"Except for the freaked-out part, yeah."

"What did he do?"

"Nothing. I don't know. His sister's getting married, and I don't want to marry him and I wish that we were like James and Tamara, but we're just not, you know?"

"Hold on. Did he ask you to marry him?" Josh asked, his usual mellow voice sounding shocked.

"No."

"Okay, so you just came to the conclusion that you don't want to marry him and you don't think your relationship has what James and Tamara's does."

"Yes."

"Okay, here's what I think you should do."

"I'm listening."

"Nothing."

"Excuse me?"

"Don't do anything. Have dinner, go home, and then call me. You're obviously upset. Don't do anything until we can figure out what's going on and what you really want to do about it."

"You're probably right," she said.

"And if I'm not, we'll deal with that too," he said.

She closed her eyes and felt herself calming down. "Thanks, Josh, I don't know what I'd do without you."

"You'll never have to find out."

After she hung up with Josh, she dried her face, put on a fake smile, and walked back to the table. The food had already arrived and Kurt was eating.

"You okay?"

"Fine," she said.

"Candace, I've been doing a lot of thinking."

"About what?" she asked, getting that sick feeling in her stomach back.

"Us. I didn't want to do this here, but I need to say this before I lose my nerve."

Please, don't let him propose! she prayed.

"I think we should break up."

She stared at him, and then burst out in hysterical laughter.

"What's so funny?" he asked.

She couldn't decide if he looked hurt or angry. "Sorry," she said. "It's just, I was thinking about the same thing."

"You were?" he asked. He seemed surprised and definitely upset by that.

She nodded.

"Why?"

"It doesn't matter," she said.

"It does to me."

"Well, then you first. Why are you breaking up with me?" she asked.

"I don't want to talk about it."

Silence stretched between them. Suddenly she really wasn't hungry, and she wanted to be anywhere else. She stood up and handed him some money. "See you around," she said, and then turned and walked outside so he wouldn't see her crying.

An hour later she was sitting on her couch downstairs, head buried against Josh's shoulder, and she was still crying. "I don't get it. I knew it was over; I wanted to break up with him. Why am I so upset?" she asked.

"Even when you know you should break up, that doesn't make it easy," Josh said. "You invested several months in him. There were obviously a lot of things you liked about him or it wouldn't have lasted this long."

She nodded. Everything he said made sense. It also hurt to get dumped. If she had broken up with Kurt, though, she'd probably feel guilty. Maybe it was better to hurt.

"So, I hear you're having a slumber party for your birthday," Josh said, clearly trying to get her mind onto different things.

"Yup," she nodded. "If everyone can come, there's going to be six of us. I've been to a couple of slumber parties, but I've never hosted one."

"Are guys invited?" Josh teased.

"No! No boys allowed," Candace said firmly.

"You're so mean."

"Yes, I'm the mean one," she said, rolling her eyes and grabbing another tissue from the box.

"So, what are you going to do at this girls-only club meeting?"

"Eat junk food, play games, and talk about boys."

"We can't come, but we can get talked about? Doesn't seem fair."

She thought about hitting him with a pillow, but it seemed like too much effort.

"It's more than fair," she said.

"So, no freezing each other's underwear? I thought that's what girls did at slumber parties."

Candace smiled. "We threaten it a lot, but I'm not sure how often that actually happens. We're more likely to play Truth or Dare."

"Oh to be a fly on the wall during that game," he said with a grin.

She was glad she had called Josh when she got home. He always seemed to be able to cheer her up. Why couldn't Kurt have been more like Josh?

The next morning at church, Candace and Tamara met up.

"You look so in love," Candace sighed.

"And you look so . . . not," Tamara said.

"What happened?" they asked each other simultaneously.

"Bad news before good," Tamara urged.

"Kurt broke up with me."

"What? You're kidding!"

"Nope. The irony was, I was seriously considering breaking up with him."

Candace briefly outlined the events of the night before.

"Do you want me to beat him up?" Tamara asked at the end.

"No."

"Can I anyway?"

"No!"

"Fine."

"So, tell me about your date," Candace said.

"Not sure that would be nice," Tamara said.

"Come on, let me at least live vicariously through your adventures."

"He took me out to the Hobbit Hole for dinner."

"Wow, I've never even been there," Candace said. It was a very upscale restaurant that only served a few tables each night.

"Me either!"

"Now that is impressive," Candace said, managing a smile. She could have sworn that Tamara had been to all the best restaurants around.

"It was very romantic, and the food was amazing."

"And?"

"And then he took me to Scandia."

Candace burst out laughing. Scandia was an amusement area that featured miniature golf, laser tag, bumper boats, and mini racecars.

"I can just see you trying to get into one of those racecars wearing that dress!" Candace said.

"It was practically impossible! I ended up with my dress almost around my waist. I beat him, though."

"Good, he deserved it," Candace said, still giggling at the image. "Please don't tell me you went on the bumper boats!"

"Nope. I put my foot down. On his, if memory serves," Tamara said, looking smug.

"Well, sounds like you had a much better evening than I did."

"Yeah. Sorry."

"Don't be sorry. It's not your fault Kurt and I aren't right for each other."

Tamara nodded. "Oh, and look what James gave me," she said, turning so Candace could see the necklace that she was wearing. Two gold hearts were intertwined on a slender chain. It was beautiful.

Candace sighed. She wanted perfect, but she'd settle for beautiful. When church was over, they headed to the youth building for Sunday school.

When they walked in, Candace spotted Jen, a freshman girl whom she had made friends with, and approached her.

"Hi, Candace," Jen said.

Candace invited her to her slumber party, and the other girl accepted eagerly.

"Are you going to invite everyone from the Bible study?" Tamara asked as they took their seats.

"Nope, just her."

"Rumor has it a new round of Bible studies is going to be starting up soon. I'm betting they'll want you to lead another one."

"Yes, because I did so well with the Christmas one," Candace said sarcastically.

"You did. Everyone said so."

"I'm too busy right now, but I totally think you should lead one," Candace said.

"Not me," Tamara said, folding her arms across her chest. "They'll just have to find another guinea pig."

"Not this guinea pig. I'm completely booked."

"School, work, play rehearsals, that's what I call overbooked."

Candace had to agree.

At school, her drama class had been rehearsing for a few weeks already for the production of *Man of La Mancha* they would be putting on. Candace still couldn't believe she had landed the lead role of Aldonza. She was pleased that after a few short weeks, even she could tell her singing was improving. Mr. Bailey seemed pleased too.

"Now, everyone, take a stack of fliers and go out there and put them up on anything that will stand still," he instructed. "Also make sure you take a ticket order form and get your friends and families signed up."

Candace stared at the ticket order form in her hand and wondered who she should invite. A few weeks ago she wouldn't have wanted anyone to come see her make an idiot of herself. As the performances drew closer, she found herself getting more excited about the whole thing.

"We also could use a few extra pair of hands to help us with set building in the next few weeks. So, if you've got friends you can beg, bribe, or bully into helping, hop to it."

The bell rang, and Candace turned to Tamara. "So, are you going to make James help?"

"No, I'm going to strongly *encourage* him to help," Tamara said with a smile.

"Nice. I've been on the receiving end of encouragement from you; he doesn't stand a chance."

"Not if he wants to live."

Tamara dropped Candace off at The Zone. As she walked toward the Candy Counter, she felt a lot more relaxed than she had on Saturday. She even allowed herself to stop and stare up at the sign for a moment. "My name's Candy too," she whispered.

She walked inside and was greeted enthusiastically by her new coworkers.

"So, where do I start?" she asked.

"Traci will show you," one of the women said.

Traci was one of the only people Candace actually remembered from Saturday. They were roughly the same age. Traci walked over and shook Candace's hand. "Let's get to work."

Traci took Candace into the kitchen area, and after they both thoroughly washed their hands, she gave her an orientation. The kitchen was massive and immaculate. Everything had its own place, and Candace's head spun as she wondered how she would keep track of it all.

"The most important thing is to clean as you go, so you'll always have utensils and equipment available when you need them," Traci explained.

"Sounds like what my mom says," Candace admitted.

"I know. I never cleaned up my dishes until I started working here," Traci said with a laugh. "Three weeks here and you won't be able to stand the sight of a dirty pan."

"My mom will want to thank you personally," Candace said.

"It happens. Every time we get a note from a family member, we frame them and put them up in the storage area. We've got several thanking us for teaching cleanliness, but quite a few more thanking us for teaching people how to cook."

"Yeah, I bet that would make a lot of husbands happy," Candace said.

"Boyfriends too. Sorry to hear about you and Kurt by the way," Traci said.

Candace thought about being surprised, but the truth was she was getting used to the fact that news traveled around The Zone lightning fast.

"It's okay. It just frees me up to find the guy of my dreams," Candace said.

"I love it."

"So, what do we make here?" Candace asked, hoping to change the subject.

"Fudge, taffies, peanut brittle, truffles, you name it. Our specialty, though, is our candy apples."

"I'm not surprised," Candace said.

"Oh, have you had one before?"

"No, it's just that I seem to gravitate to everything *candy* in this park."

"Because of your name?"

Candace nodded.

"Well, it could be worse."

"How?"

"You could be Pat Moptop."

"Who is Pat Moptop?" Candace asked.

"She started out as a sweeper, now she cleans the referee restrooms. Basically, she's always mopping up."

"You're messing with me," Candace accused.

"Nope, honest."

"Then you're right. It could be a lot worse. Tell me more about the candy apples."

"Well, we coat the candy apples in sugar and cinnamon, and then we have fun. We can put all sorts of different candies and chocolate on them. We also make caramel and chocolate caramel apples. Those come with and without nuts."

Before Candace could say anything, the kitchen doors burst open. She turned and saw Gib and Roger come in, followed by a couple other Muffin Mansion employees. Roger was dressed similarly to the others with the exception that his shirt was all white. She couldn't help but stare at the blank shirt. All referee shirts had a stripe, no matter how subtle.

"Oh, no," Traci whispered beside her.

"What's going on?" Candace asked.

"You'll see."

"Why is Roger's shirt white?" Candace asked.

"Because he needs to earn his stripes," Gib growled. "Until then, no stripes."

He sounded so fierce, Candace found herself backing away from him.

"Now look here, you galley rat," Gib said, clearly addressing Roger. "If you want to work at the Muffin Mansion, then you have to prove your worth."

"Sir, yes, sir," Roger tried to shout. It came out as barely more than a whisper.

"Take a good look around you. Notice everything about this place. I'll give you sixty seconds. Go."

Roger raced around the room. Candace watched in fascination as he opened cupboards, counted ovens and inspected the storage area. He looked like a madman. He came back front and center just in time for Gib to call time.

"Close your eyes," Gib ordered.

Roger did as he was told.

"Now, tell me the five biggest differences between this kitchen and the one at the Muffin Mansion."

"There are two more ovens here, but all of the ovens are smaller than the Muffin Mansion."

"Go on."

"No beakers, test tubes, Bunsen burners, or any other scientific equipment."

"Continue."

"Flour is stacked in the storage area instead of being dispensed from a barrel."

"What else?"

"Only one sink here instead of three."

"And the last?"

Roger went completely pale. "I-I-don't know."

"Open your eyes," Gib growled.

Roger did, flinching when he saw the angry expression on Gib's face that was only inches from his own.

"What is the fifth thing?" Roger asked.

"It's clean!" Gib bellowed.

The forcefulness in his voice caused Candace to back up until she bumped into one of the refrigerators.

"And do you know why that is?" Gib asked.

"Because I don't work here?" Roger suggested.

"That's right! Every pan clean all the time. And when you knock over the flour, clean it up! Don't stand there writing love notes in it."

Candace bit her lip to keep from laughing.

4

The next day Candace and her team met to decide how they were going to handle Talent Show. Pete and Sue she knew well. Traci she was getting to know, but Corinne was a mystery. What on earth could they all do together for the talent show?

"Okay, so what is our talent?" Candace asked the small group. She looked around and saw only blank stares. "There has to be something we could be good at."

"I'm good at running trains, but I'm not sure how that would be a demonstrable talent," Pete said.

"Okay, but at least that's a talent," Candace encouraged.

"Don't you act?" Traci asked. "You said something about being in a play."

"Not in public ... yet," Candace said. "But let's pick something we can all get behind."

"I can chew gum and blow really big bubbles," Corinne said.

"Yeah, then they can watch me clean it up," Sue said with a frustrated sigh.

"Seriously, there has to be something. What are the other groups doing?"

"I heard the Muffin Mansion is recreating the finale from *The Lord of the Dance*," Traci said.

"I didn't know Gib could do Irish dancing," Candace said, for a moment distracted from her mission by trying to picture him dressed up like Michael Flatley.

"I think it's Becca's thing," Traci said. "They're calling it *The* Lady *of the Dance*."

That at least made sense.

"What about singing?" Corinne suggested.

"You don't want to hear that from me," Sue said.

"Or me," Pete added.

"A couple of guys from the Dug Out are doing that whole comedy routine, 'Who's on First?' " Traci said.

"And I saw a group practicing juggling," Corinne said.

"What are the Kowabunga guys doing?" Candace asked.

"No one knows," Pete said. "They're keeping it real quiet."

"Okay, so we know what some of the other groups are doing, but what can we do?"

"Maybe we could twirl fire batons," Sue said with a smirk.

"Or play water goblets," Traci said.

"Okay, enough with Sandra Bullock and *Miss Congeniality*. We're not in a beauty pageant. We need a group activity that we can either all do or learn," Candace said.

A breeze kicked up and knocked over several of the plastic cups. Corinne reached out and grabbed them, then stacked them into a pyramid before breaking them back down and stacking them in a tower.

Candace watched fascinated as Corinne's hands flew around the cups. The clacking sound they made as she stacked them was somehow soothing. "Where did you learn to do that?" she asked.

"What? Oh, the cups?"

"Yeah."

"Slow days at food service. You do anything to beat the boredom. You know there's a whole new sport that's sprung up around stacking cups. Lots of bored fast-food workers in the world, I guess," Corinne said.

"That's it!" Candace said.

"What?" Sue asked.

"Corinne can teach us all to stack cups."

Traci looked at her like she was crazy, but Pete caught on. "With ten hands I bet we could make all kinds of interesting shapes pretty quickly," he said.

"Exactly. Corinne said it, it's become a sport."

"I'm not good enough to compete in the sport," Corinne said.

"But you are good enough to compete in a talent show. And with your help, we will be too," Candace said.

That night Candace went online and was surprised to discover that cup stacking actually was a sport. It was mostly played by children. On YouTube she saw videos of some of the top competitors in the world. She couldn't even follow what they were doing with their hands. The pattern they were doing was called the cycle.

"Okay, I know I can't get fast enough to be impressive, but I'm guessing we can do something big and that might look even cooler," she said out loud.

At any rate it was worth a try. Hopefully none of the other teams had the same idea.

The next couple of days passed by in a blur of work and school. Candace was grateful that she hadn't seen Kurt at the park. She was even more grateful that she hadn't seen Lisa. She wasn't sure what she would do if Lisa tried to taunt her. Then again, she often thought that Kurt and Lisa could already be back together once she was out of the way.

After only a few short shifts, she and Traci had gotten to be friends. Compared to most Zone referees, the crew who worked at the Candy Counter seemed pretty mellow. It was almost a disappointment. But when she caught a glimpse of Roger in Muffin Mansion training, she was relieved.

The day of the slumber party finally arrived, and Candace spent the whole day feeling hyper and slightly out of control. She put it down to Becca's influence. Candace was excited. She had never had enough friends to have a slumber party before. Her birthdays had usually consisted of doing something with her parents, Tamara, and possibly a couple other relatives.

After school, Tamara and Candace picked up the ice-cream cake and headed back to Candace's house where her mom had gone all out on decorations. There were balloons and streamers everywhere. Apparently her mom was also excited about the big party.

Becca was the first to arrive, followed closely by Jen and Traci. Sue was the last to arrive, but she had a look of triumph on her face when she came through the doors.

"Sibs are both at sleepovers," she explained. "I'm so looking forward to this."

Candace hugged her.

"Okay, let's get started!" Candace said. "First up we've got some games."

They played several individual and relay-race games. Some Candace remembered from other parties. Others had been suggested to her by Josh who seemed to have an endless knowledge of party games. They ended with charades, which Candace, Traci, and Jen won.

After cake and presents, her parents headed upstairs for the night.

"Hey, can we turn on the Escape! Channel for just a second?" Becca asked.

"Sure," Candace said, turning on the TV. "What's on?"

"I just want to see which of my sister's shows is on tonight."

"Your sister?" Tamara asked.

"Yeah, Bunni Sinclair. She works for the Escape! Channel."

"As in *Bunni's Best*?" Jen asked excitedly.

"Yeah."

"I love her shows!" Jen said, grabbing Becca's arm. "You have to get me her autograph."

"Sure," Becca said with a smile.

Candace flipped to the Escape! Channel. A middle-aged man with white hair was screaming and running through a creepy-looking house chased by a guy with a night-vision camera.

"That's the ghost guy," Jen said.

"He screams like a girl," Traci said.

The show ended and a minute later a pretty, blonde woman with a strong resemblance to Becca filled the screen. An announcer said, "Tonight, 'Bunni's Best Backpacking Equipment.' "

"It's a repeat. You can turn it off," Becca said.

An advertisement came on, and it was Bunni. "I'm Bunni Sinclair for the Escape! Channel, and you're watching 'Bunni's Best.' Coming up after my show, 'Girl Meets Guam.' " Bunni's nose twitched.

" 'Girl Meets Guam'? That oughta be good," Tamara smirked.

"They're all crazy over there," Becca said.

"I just can't believe your sister's on television," Candace said.

Becca shrugged.

Candace turned off the TV.

"Okay, Truth or Dare!" Tamara shouted. Everyone formed a circle on the floor.

"Jen, truth or dare," Tamara said.

"Umm ... truth?"

"Who do you want to marry?"

"That's easy. The Jonas Brothers."

"Which one?" Candace asked.

"All of them," Jen said with a dreamy smile.

"Okay, so we have one polygamist among us," Tamara laughed. "Your turn."

"Okay, Candace, truth or dare," Jen said.

Candace hesitated. It wasn't like she didn't trust the girls who were there. They were all friends, but she wasn't sure what Jen might ask her. "Dare."

"I dare you to drink that bottle of Coke," Jen said, pointing to a 2-liter bottle that was almost full.

Candace groaned. "This is going to hurt," she said. She stood up and got the bottle. "Can I pour it in a cup and take my time?" she asked hopefully.

"Nope, straight from the bottle, and you've got five minutes."

Candace felt naughty drinking straight out of the bottle. She sat down on the ground and hefted the bottle. Fortunately the Coke was still cold. About halfway through she took a breather and sat gasping for a minute.

"You got one minute left!" Tamara said.

Candace swallowed faster. She emptied the bottle and set it down right as Tamara called time. Her stomach felt like the liquid was sloshing around in it, and she groaned.

"That was impressive," Becca said, eyes envious.

Candace saluted her. "Okay, Becca, truth or dare."

"I'll take the soda please," Becca said, eyes wide.

"Sorry, different dare, one that doesn't involve sugar. So, truth or dare?"

"Truth," Becca said, looking supremely disappointed.

"How's Roger as a kisser?"

Becca blushed fiercely. "Good. Very sweet and very passionate. It's like he can read my mind, and he knows just how to kiss me at any given time."

"Lucky," Traci said. "My boyfriend is all tongue all the time. It's so gross."

They all squealed in response and then started laughing.

"Sue, truth or dare?" Becca asked.

"Truth."

"What do you find most attractive in a guy?"

"Great, broad shoulders, the broader the better. Unless you were talking about nonphysical stuff, then I'd have to say 'sweet.' "

"Boo on the sweet, too boring," Tamara said, tossing a pillow at Sue.

Sue caught the pillow. "It's true. I like sweet guys. Traci, truth or dare?"

"Dare, definitely."

"I've got a good one," Sue said, "but only if Candace says it's okay."

"What is it?" Candace asked.

"Traci has to sneak upstairs, pound on your parents' door, and make it back downstairs without them seeing her."

"No way!" Traci said.

Tamara burst out laughing and fell over, clutching her sides.

"I used to do that to my parents when I had slumber parties," Sue said.

"And they didn't ground you for life?" Jen marveled.

Candace was pretty sure her parents would be cool about it, but she was also sure they'd want some warning.

"Well?" Becca asked.

"Let me think about it for a minute while I go to the bathroom," Candace said, jumping to her feet. "Too much soda."

Candace made her way upstairs and then knocked softly on her parents' door before going in. They were both still awake.

"Sounds like fun down there," her dad said.

"It is, thank you," she said.

"Then why are you up here?" her mom asked.

Candace explained to them what was going on.

"I swear I didn't say anything to anyone," Candace's mom said to her dad.

"What?"

"Your mom used to do the same thing to your grandparents," her dad said with a chuckle. "It's fine by me as long as we have a two a.m. moratorium on banging."

"You guys rock," Candace said before scooting out of the room and down the hall to the bathroom.

A minute later she rejoined the others in the living room. "What did I miss?"

"We're laying the ground rules," Becca said.

"Traci has to pound five times on the door," Tamara said.

"And all of us have to stand at the top of the stairs and watch her," Jen said.

"If Candace says it's okay," Sue reminded.

They all turned to her, and Candace nodded solemnly. They got up and crept toward the stairs as a group. They were about halfway up when Candace whispered to Tamara, "Did you tell them my dad has a terrible temper?"

Tamara looked at her like she had lost her mind.

"No, but maybe I should have," Tamara said, struggling to play along.

"I'm not doing this!" Traci hissed, and started to back down the stairs.

The rest of them pushed forward until they were at the top of the stairs.

"I want truth!" Traci said.

"Too late!" Sue said.

Candace felt sorry for the other girl and for a moment toyed with letting her off the hook. But she couldn't bring herself to do it. The whole thing was so funny, including the look of fear on her friends' faces.

Candace pointed to her parents' door, and Traci crept forward toward it.

"Remember, five times," Sue whispered.

Even Candace's heart was pounding when Traci lifted her hand. She swung her fist, but before it could land, the door flew open. Light blazed out around her father.

Everyone screamed and went running and sliding back down the stairs. Someone stepped on Candace's foot, but they all kept going. When they reached the living room, they slid into fake sleeping positions on the floor like that could somehow save them.

Her dad must have been jumping on the stairs because each footfall seemed to shake the house. He was like the mighty ogre come to punish them.

"Having a good birthday?" Tamara whispered.

Candace reached out and squeezed her hand. "The best."

"I know you're not sleeping!" her father said.

It took all of Candace's self-control not to burst out laughing. She bit her lip as her dad stalked around for a minute. He finally turned and went back upstairs. When they heard the door close behind him, they all broke into giggles.

Everyone sat up except for Traci. For a moment Candace thought the other girl had fallen asleep or fainted or something, but she could see her eyelids fluttering.

"Is Traci asleep?" Becca asked.

"Only one way to find out," Jen said.

"I think it's time to freeze her bra," Candace added.

Traci sat straight up, and Candace fell over laughing.

5

Sunday morning her mom came into the room and woke Candace up, handing her the phone. "Martha from The Zone," her mom explained.

"Martha? I don't work Sundays," Candace said groggily.

"I know, that's why I had to call you at home," Martha said with a chuckle. "Tomorrow afternoon I need you to wear a suit and report to the Party Zone at four."

"Why?"

"Several news channels are going to be there to do a piece on the five scholarship finalists."

"What?" Candace asked, coming fully awake.

"You're going to be on the news, so wear something nice."

Candace groaned. "I'm not ready for this."

"I would be surprised if you thought you were," Martha said. "You'll be great, I know it. Remember, tomorrow at four. I'll see you there."

Martha hung up before Candace could protest. She sat there for a second before leaping out of bed and racing down the hall. "Mom! I need you!"

Candace nervously smoothed down her navy blue skirt. She straightened the jacket, trying not to dislodge the tiny microphone one of the news crew had pinned on it. She had pulled her hair back in a barrette, and one of the strands was pulled painfully tight. She thought about taking it down and putting it back but was afraid she would just make it worse. She checked her lipstick for the third time, using her cell phone camera since she didn't have a mirror. Around her the other finalists seemed equally agitated.

The news crew finished setting up, and the five were directed to chairs lined up together. Candace sat on the far right, wishing there was a way she could just slide out of the frame and not be seen.

She recognized one of the reporters from KTLA, which did nothing to calm her nerves. Somehow knowing who one of the reporters was just made it that much more real. Someone handed her a cup of water, and she drank it, more because it gave her something to do than because she was thirsty.

She caught a glimpse of John Hanson as a makeup woman checked his hair and straightened his microphone.

"Someone needs to remember to breathe," a familiar voice said in her ear.

Candace looked over her shoulder. Josh was bent down, arm on the back of her chair.

"Breathe," she said, reminding herself to do so. Then she tilted her head upward and looked into Josh's eyes and promptly forgot again. She began to feel warm, and she blushed.

"Okay, we're live in two," one of the cameramen shouted.

Candace shook herself and turned back to face the cameras. They suddenly seemed a lot less scary than continuing to look at Josh. She stared at the KTLA reporter as the woman stepped in front of the camera.

Then they were on the air.

"I'm here at The Zone where today marks a very special day, not only for the park, but also for some very lucky referees. Today is the fifteenth anniversary of the park's opening."

Just another thing I'm the last to know, Candace thought to herself.

"And they're taking Zone-style celebrations to a whole new level. Here at The Zone, season ticket holders are in for a year of fun and surprises. Here with me to explain some of this is the park's founder, John Hanson. John, what can you tell us about what you've got planned for this year?"

"Well, we're excited to introduce some new rides and merchandise. Our biggest innovation is Player Stats. Now, season ticket holders have the chance to swipe their tickets at different rides and special events and get their own customized stats and trading cards."

"Sounds pretty amazing!"

"We're always working on new ways of making the game better for our players here at The Zone. This is just one of many new things we're unveiling this year."

"Guess I'll have to renew my season ticket," the reporter said.

"Already taken care of," John said, handing her a card. "And here's your initial trading card."

"It looks better than I do," the reporter joked. "Now, let's meet some other Zone celebrities. John who do we have with us?"

John turned and indicated Candace and the four other referees. "These five referees are the final nominees for The Zone scholarship. Each of them has designed a potential new ride and earned the esteem of their colleagues. The winner receives a full scholarship to Florida Coast where they will study one of the disciplines conducive to becoming a Game Master."

"Let's meet the finalists," the reporter said, moving toward Candace. "Tell us a little bit about yourself and your ride."

"My name is Candace Thompson. I really don't feel like I belong here, but I'm grateful to be considered. My ride idea is called Balloon Races. It's from a sketch I made, and a friend entered me in the contest."

"Sounds like quite a friend."

"Yes, he is," Candace said, starting to blush again.

The reporter moved on to the guy sitting next to Candace, and it was all she could do not to sag in relief. A couple minutes later the reporter signed off, and the cameras shut down.

"You were awesome!" Josh said, reappearing behind her.

"I'm shaking," Candace commented, staring at her own trembling fingers in fascination.

"No one could tell."

"Thank you, Josh. It was really cool of you to enter me in the contest."

"See, I knew you'd see it my way sooner or later," he joked.

"Wonderful job, everyone!" John Hanson said, beaming at everyone.

Breathe. Just breathe.

"This year the winner will be announced at the conclusion of Talent Show," he continued.

Great. Something more to be nervous about on that day. That was so not what she needed. She turned to Josh, eager to change the subject.

"So, I'm behind on all the special anniversary stuff apparently," Candace said.

"You know, there is a referee website. You can keep up with everything there," Josh said.

"Oh great, I've worked here nearly a year and this is the first I've heard of it."

"Who on earth handled your orientation?" Josh asked.

"All I remember was that he seemed psycho, and he moved really fast for being that overweight."

Josh laughed. "Should have known. Remind me, and one of these days I'll give you the full tour."

"I'd like that," Candace said.

"Candace, that was so cool!" Sue said, walking over.

"Thanks!" Candace said, standing to hug her. "I was so nervous."

"I couldn't tell," Mark said appearing next to Josh.

"You guys are sweet," Candace said.

"Hi, I'm Sue," Sue said, offering her hand to Mark.

He shook it and seemed only to have eyes for her. "Check."

"Your name's Check?"

"No, it's Mark."

"Mark. Good to meet you, Mark."

"You too."

Candace rolled her eyes. What was the deal? Everyone she knew was falling in love and finding their soul mate at The Zone. Why hadn't that worked out for her?

"Candace."

"Yes?" she said, turning to Josh.

"Let's get out of here and get some pizza."

"You're buying."

"Totally," he said with a grin.

"Seriously, what is the big secret?" Candace asked.

"Come on, you know my big secret," Josh said.

"Not *that* secret. The other one. You know, the one that has to do with Talent Show?"

"Oh, that secret. You mean you want me to betray the trust of my fellow Kowabunga refs and tell you what we're planning?"

"Well, when you put it that way ... yes."

"No!" he laughed. "I did hear rumors though about a certain group and cup stacking?"

She stuck her tongue out at him.

"So it is true! Well, it's certainly ... unique."

"Don't knock it. I bet we can beat whatever your group has cooked up."

"Do I hear the start of another bet?" Josh asked.

"You're on."

"Same terms as before?"

"Loser buys pizza for the winner's team," Candace affirmed.

They shook on it.

"Now will you please tell me what your talent is?"

"You're just going to have to wait and see it with everyone else."

"You are so mean to me."

Their pizza arrived and they dug in. After a minute Josh looked at her thoughtfully. "So, have you had a chance to talk to Kurt?"

Candace shook her head. "I don't like the way we left things. I'd like some closure, you know, find out what he thought went wrong."

"So, what's the problem?"

"Part of me really doesn't want to know," she admitted.

"Whatever it was, it couldn't have been anything you did," Josh said, leaning toward her.

"I don't know. I'm sure I could have been a better girlfriend."

"He could have been a better boyfriend."

"I guess it goes both ways. It's just weird. Everyone around me seems to be falling in love."

"Ah, you noticed the Sue-Checkmark sparks too?"

"More like fireworks."

Josh shrugged. "It's spring. Everyone's falling in love."

"At least Tamara and James had the decency to fall in love during the winter."

Josh grinned. "Roger and Becca probably fell in love over the summer."

"That's true."

"So really Sue and Mark are the only offenders."

Candace laughed. "Not necessarily the word I would have chosen, but I guess you're right."

"It's okay, Candace. I know there's a guy somewhere who's perfect for you."

For some reason she couldn't bring herself to look him in the eyes while she nodded.

Candace swallowed hard as she stared at the letter in her hand. It was the moment of truth. The return address identified the letter as coming from UCLA. She and Tamara had both applied there. It had been her backup college choice for so long she had begun to think of it at some point as her primary choice.

What if they don't want me? she wondered. *What will I do?*

She took a deep breath and tore it open. The page was crowded with type, and her eyes blurred as she tried to pick out a word that would tell her at a glance if the news was good or bad.

She wiped a hand across her eyes and struggled to bring the words into focus. *Inform.* That was a neutral word. It could mean anything. *Unfortunately.* Her stomach did a flip-flop. That was definitely a bad word. Then her eyes saw *pleased.* A good word if ever there was one.

We are pleased to inform you that you have been accepted . . .

She shrieked at the top of her lungs, and her parents came running from the kitchen.

"I got into UCLA!"

Suddenly they were all hugging and jumping up and down. It was five minutes before Candace actually read the rest of the letter. *Unfortunately* turned out to be *Unfortunately, we cannot offer you a scholarship at this time.* That was okay. Her parents had already agreed to pick up the tab for college in-state with out-of-state negotiable.

"Congratulations," her mom said finally.

"Well, the backup plan is firmly in place," her dad said with a smile. "Not that I ever doubted it for a minute."

Candace had, but she was too embarrassed to admit it.

"Are you going to call Tamara?" her dad asked.

"You have to tell Josh too," her mom said.

"Okay, I'll make some calls," Candace said.

She gave her parents one more hug before dashing upstairs. She called Tamara first.

"Hello?"

"Tam, guess what!" Candace squealed.

"I have no clue, but I'm guessing it's good."

"I got into UCLA!"

"Congratulations, I knew you would."

"Thanks. Have you heard anything yet?"

"Not yet," Tamara admitted.

"Oh," Candace said, suddenly feeling worried for her friend. Then again it was Tamara. Anything she wanted she got. There was no way she wasn't getting in. "Well, you'll probably get yours in a couple of days."

"They send those things out in waves over several weeks," Tamara said.

"That's right. Plus, I turned my application in before you did."

"Totally. No worries," Tamara said, her voice breezy. "I did get my acceptance letter from Loyola today."

"Oh, that's wonderful! That's a good school."

"Yeah, but I'm going to UCLA. Maybe we can room together," Tamara said, getting excited.

"Yeah, if I go to UCLA. Totally."

"If? When did UCLA become an if?" Tamara asked.

"Oh, well, if I end up winning the scholarship, I guess I'll be going to Florida Coast."

There was a long pause on the other end, and for a second Candace thought they had been disconnected.

"Tam?"

"You know I'm not cool with that, right?"

"With what?" Candace asked even though she could guess the answer.

"Florida. I'm not cool with you going to college on the opposite coast."

Candace bit her lip. It was a fight she'd been hoping to avoid … possibly forever. "Tam, can we cross that bridge when we get to it?"

"Yeah," Tam said with a sigh.

"Cool."

"Okay, go tell the rest of the world the good news."

"You too."

Candace hung up and then dialed Josh.

"Yes, Candace?" he answered the phone.

"You know, you're supposed to say 'hi' first," she teased.

"My way is faster. What's up?"

"I got my acceptance letter to UCLA."

"Congratulations. At least they recognize what they're going to be missing when you go to Florida Coast."

"Josh, the only way I'm going to Florida Coast is if I get the scholarship."

"Which I think you will."

"Thanks for the vote of confidence, but I'm not holding my breath."

"Okay, but don't say I didn't tell you," Josh said.

"I promise. So, have you gotten any letters yet?"

"I got the Florida Coast acceptance letter a few minutes ago."

"Awesome!"

"Yup."

"So, which ones are you waiting on?"

"None, that's the only one I applied to," he said.

"Seriously?"

"Seriously."

"Well, I guess there's no decision-making for you at this point."

"Nope, already sweated all that out."

"Must be nice."

"More like anticlimactic, but it's cool. When you know what you want, that's all you need."

"I guess that's true," she admitted.

"So, Florida Coast and UCLA. Where else did you apply?" he asked.

"UC San Diego and UC Irvine."

"Have a UC fixation?" he teased.

"My folks promised to pay for any school in-state."

"Then you should have gone for Stanford."

She laughed. "I'm not a genius, and I don't have perfect grades. Somehow I think Stanford's beyond my reach."

"That's the difference between you and me."

"Stanford's not out of your reach?"

"I think you can achieve anything you want, and you just don't know it yet."

"Oh. Thank you," Candace said.

It was nice that Josh thought so highly of her, but it was also deeply intimidating. She didn't want to let him down. Somehow his believing in her made her want to try harder, do more, and be better. It was an awesome responsibility.

"You're welcome," he said.

It was weird, but there was a moment when she could swear he understood everything that she had been thinking. She smiled.

"Okay, go make your calls, and I'll make my calls."

"We should celebrate," she said.

"I'm all for that. Unfortunately not tonight. I'm practicing with my team."

Candace sighed. "Foiled by the talent show."

"Just get used to saying that," he teased. "How about Friday?"

"My Friday is yours," she said.

"Awesome, I'm going to hold you to that."

6

Candace, Sue, Pete, Traci, and Corinne were gathered around Sue's dining table. Josh's constant goading about the talent show had taken its toll, and Candace had pushed for practice for their team. It was their first practice, and she had fully expected it to go badly ... just not as badly as it was actually going.

On the table they had five sets of stacking cups. They each stood at their own station as Corinne tried to show them for the fiftieth time how to stack them quickly into simple pyramids. Even Sue was getting frustrated and looked like she was about two seconds from exploding.

"Okay, forget all the other cups, just take three cups," Corinne said. "Put two of them upside down touching each other and balance the third one on top."

Each of them did as instructed. For once they all balanced, and Candace lifted her hands away nervously from her little pyramid. "Victory!" she joked.

"Good," Corinne said. "Now take hold of the top cup and push it down and to the right until it stacks on top of the right base cup."

Pete, Sue, and Candace succeeded. Traci's cups ended up on the floor. She flopped down beside them. "I give," she wailed.

"We've made progress," Candace said, trying to be optimistic.

"I think we should pick a different talent," Corinne sighed.

"We don't have any other talent; we've established that," Pete said.

Sue burst out laughing. "We're in serious trouble."

Candace sat down next to Traci. "At least we each managed a pyramid. That's progress."

"We're going to need a whole lot more than that to keep from getting laughed off the stage," Pete said.

"Is it too late to reconsider the acting thing?" Sue asked. "I know Candace has been rehearsing to be in *Man of La Mancha.* Maybe we could all act out a scene or sing a song or something."

"Who are you playing?" Pete asked.

"Aldonza."

"The lead, that's cool," Traci said.

"It's scary," Candace admitted.

"Why?" Corinne asked.

"I don't want to make a fool of myself on stage in front of thousands of people, some of whom I know."

"I'm confused. Are we talking about *Man of La Mancha* or the talent show?" Sue quipped.

"Yes," Candace said. "They both freak me out."

"I don't get that," Traci said.

"You don't get stage fright?" Pete asked.

"No, I get that generally, but I don't get Candace. I mean, you're constantly in the limelight in some way. Aren't you used to it?"

Candace laughed. "Believe it or not, I was never anywhere near a light, lime or otherwise, until I started working at The Zone. The last year has been crazy. I'm not sure how I keep ending up on stages or front and center, but it sure isn't getting any easier."

"I'd love to be in your shoes," Corinne said wistfully.

"Seriously?" Candace asked.

The other girl nodded.

A couple months before, Candace would have offered to switch places with her. Now, though, things were changing. Just because she was scared stiff to be in the spotlight, didn't mean she was ready to give it up. Even that scared her, but it had to be progress. She'd had enough people lecture her about not hiding in the shadows, she had started to think there was something to it.

Maybe Josh was right. Maybe she would win the scholarship. It would certainly track with the way her life had been going. Florida Coast seemed like a world away from her life and her comfort zone. But everything that had happened to her in the last year had been pushing her from that comfort zone. She was beginning to think that God was trying to tell her something.

"Penny for your thoughts," Sue said.

Candace smiled. "I think with a little more practice we could win this thing."

"You're crazy," Traci said, staring at her.

"It's been said before, and it might even be true," Candace answered. "But I think we've got all the skill we need, we just need to put a little determination behind it."

She jumped to her feet, and reluctantly Traci followed suit. They all reassembled around the table and prepared to try again.

Three hours later they called it a night. Candace's fingers were cramped up, and her back was killing her, but by the end they had each managed to make a large pyramid and break it down. Even Traci had started to feel optimistic.

Candace made it home and then staggered upstairs and fell lengthwise on her bed. She was exhausted, but she was feeling good. It was amazing how much they had gotten accomplished.

She flipped over and grabbed Mr. Huggles. She wondered how the other teams were doing. She realized she didn't even know what half of her friends were doing for their talent. Josh was still being mysterious. She hadn't had a chance to ask Martha what her team was doing. Becca, Roger, Gib, and the rest of the crew of the Muffin Mansion were doing the whole *Lord of the Dance* thing. She could just picture Becca, hyped up on sugar, her feet a blur as she moved across the stage. That was going to be something to see.

She thought about Kurt and wondered what he was doing for the talent show. She didn't even know if he was teamed up with some of his mascot friends. Then again, for all she knew, he might be teamed up with Lisa. She growled under her breath and fought back tears. She knew she and Kurt were wrong for each other. Why did it still hurt to think about him? Why did it make her angry when she thought of him dating someone else?

I need some sort of closure, she thought. *Josh was right. Then again, he usually is.*

She crawled back off the bed and changed into her pajamas. Then she climbed under the covers and started to pray. *God, help me make the right choices. There are so many paths I can take, and I'm not sure what to do. Help me to be able to let go of Kurt. Help me not to be angry with him or jealous. God, help me to find the man you created for me.*

She drifted off to sleep and dreamed about stacking cups that reached toward the heavens.

The next day Candace's victory with the stacking cups faded into the background as she faced total failure at capturing Aldonza's sense of anger at Don Quixote. She sat on the edge of the stage, legs dangling as Mr. Bailey tried to explain it to her.

"Look, she's a peasant; worse, she's a prostitute. She is nothing. She has nothing, no self-respect, nada. Along comes this guy who refuses to acknowledge the reality of her situation and then has the gall to declare that she is a lady of standing and virtue, the likes of which she has never seen let alone could ever be."

"And that makes her mad?"

"Yes, because it only makes her feel the shame of who she is that much more deeply. He thinks of her as this amazing creature, and he expects her to behave like a lady. It just makes the reality of her life that much worse."

The light slowly began to dawn. Candace thought about Josh and how he seemed to have a higher opinion of her and her abilities than she did. It was flattering, but also frightening. Sometimes she felt like a fake around him and was terrified of letting him down, of proving him wrong. She didn't want to disappoint him.

Don Quixote, for all his good intentions, made Aldonza feel terrible because she wasn't what he thought she should be.

"You're getting it," Mr. Bailey said. "I can see it in your eyes."

She nodded slowly.

"Good. Now focus on that. Bring that frustration and guilt and humiliation to bear on Don Quixote. If it weren't for him, you wouldn't have to be in so much pain."

"I am so angry, I almost hate him," she muttered.

"Exactly. But then, at the end, it is his faith in you that gives you the strength to become the woman he always thought you were. And you, in turn, restore his faith in his dream."

"That's beautiful."

"Yes, it is."

"Okay."

Mr. Bailey stepped back and clapped his hands together. "Okay, people, let's go again from the beginning of the scene."

Candace hopped to her feet and took her place. From the floor of the auditorium Tamara flashed her an encouraging smile.

"And, action!"

Candace was still running the lines in her head when she made it to work. She put her purse in a locker in the Locker Room and then exited toward the park.

She hadn't gone more than a few steps when she ran into Martha, walking with a guy a couple years older than Candace.

"Candace, there's someone I want you to meet," Martha said.

The stranger was a tall, shy-looking guy with glasses, a Zone T-shirt, and a quirky grin.

"Candace this is Gary. He's a former scholarship winner. Gary, Candace is one of our finalists."

They shook hands. "Congratulations," Gary said.

"And to you. Wow. So, what's it like winning?"

"It's awesome!"

"Talk, ask questions, Candace," Martha said, leaving with a little wave.

"So you go to Florida Coast?" Candace asked after Martha left.

"I did. I just took my last final a couple days ago."

"Wow, so what are you going to do now?"

Gary grinned. "You're looking at the newest Game Master."

"That's amazing!

"I'm totally stoked. It's amazing. Four years ago I was you. I remember how excited and freaked out I was. I wasn't even sure that this was what I wanted to do with my life."

"What happened?"

"Simple. I rode the ride I designed. It was such a rush, I can't even tell you. It was at the end of my Freshman year. After I got off the Spiral, I I knew that I wanted to make rides for a living."

"You created that? They put it up not that long ago!"

"I know," he said proudly. "I was here for the opening. They build your ride at the Florida park, and if it does well, it has a chance of coming here."

Candace was amazed. The Spiral was one of the coolest roller coasters in the park. "Your ride rocks!"

"Thanks! Just wait until you see your ride in real life."

"That's if I win," Candace said, wishing more than anything that she did. She closed her eyes for just a minute and imagined what it would be like to ride the Balloon Races. That alone would be worth the fight with Tamara when Candace told her she was for sure going to Florida Coast instead of UCLA.

"I think you're going to win," he said.

"Based on what?" Candace asked.

"You have that look to you."

"Okay, you lost me. What look would that be?"

"You look like a Zoner, like someone who could spend the rest of her life working and playing in the parks. The other four don't. Sure, they like it here and they're all interested in design, but they'd be just as happy working for Cedar Parks or Disney or any other theme park. The one guy just wants to be an architect, he's not even really interested in theme-park design."

"Really?"

"Really."

"Then I take it you're a Zoner?"

"From the first day I walked down the Home Stretch," Gary affirmed. "That was one of the best moments of my life."

"That's cool."

Gary nodded. "Look, I'm going to be around now. If you have any questions about the program or Florida Coast, just look me up. We scholarship winners tend to look out for one another."

"Thanks," she said, giving him an impromptu hug.

"No problem."

"Glad to see you're moving on," a catty voice said.

Candace pulled away just in time to see Lisa saunter by. She stuck her tongue out at Lisa's back as she passed.

"What was that all about?" Gary asked.

"Trust me, you really, really don't want to know," Candace said with a sigh.

"Actually, I do," he said.

Candace laughed. "Well, at least you admit it. That's my ex-boyfriend's ex-girlfriend."

"Messy."

"Yeah. Somehow I expected her to be nicer, or at least ignore me, now that he and I broke up."

"Some people just can't leave well enough alone. She's probably jealous of you."

"Jealous?"

"Get used to it. Going to Florida Coast on a Zone scholarship is an amazing thing. Unfortunately, you'll have classmates that will drive you crazy because of it."

"Bummer."

Gary shrugged. "You know what they say, 'what doesn't kill you makes you stronger.' "

"I could go for a little less strong," Candace sighed.

"You'll do fine, Candace."

"I'm glad you think so."

"You should think so too. Have a little more faith in yourself. From what Martha tells me, you're a real star. You just don't know it yet."

"I'm really starting to think God's trying to tell me something," Candace said to herself.

"I don't doubt it."

7

After work, Candace went looking for Becca. She discovered that most of the crew of the Muffin Mansion were rehearsing in the Party Zone. She made her way over there and saw a group of referees on the stage lined up in a straight row. In front of them, Becca paced back and forth, hands clasped behind her back, as she gave orders.

"The key to this dance is timing. Listen to the music, watch each other. If you're out of step even by a moment, the entire performance loses its impact. Now, let's take it again from the top."

She moved over to a CD player, and a moment later the finale music from *Lord of the Dance* was pouring out of its tiny speakers with surprising force. Becca raised her arms like she was a music conductor, paused for a moment, and then let them fall.

The dancers burst into movement, their feet striking the ground rhythmically and with deep thuds. Candace watched amazed as they bounced and kicked and moved seemingly as one. When it was over, she couldn't help but applaud.

"Take five," Becca instructed before hopping down off the stage. "Hey, Candace, got a little espionage thing going on here?"

"No reconnaissance, just wanted to see you," Candace said with a laugh.

"What's up?"

"Mostly I was hoping to catch you on a dinner break so we could chat. I also wanted to ask you some advice in the guy department."

"Oh," Becca said, eyes growing wide. "Gotcha. Well, if you've got some time, you can hang out for a few. We're almost done, and then we can go get some dinner."

"Sounds like a plan. You're sure you won't mind if I watch?"

Becca shrugged. "Unlike some people, we've made no secret of what we're doing."

"That's true," Candace said. "Some people are being quite the pain about it."

"I personally think it's a lack of confidence in their performance. If you can't dazzle them with brilliance, baffle them with mystery."

"I like your theory. I'll mention it to Josh."

"Please do," Becca said. "And tell him his team is going to lose."

"Ah, the competitive spirit of The Zone in full swing."

"Isn't it beautiful?" Becca asked.

She hopped back on the stage. "Okay, people, one more time ... with feeling."

Candace smiled as she watched. One thing was for sure, they were going to be the team to beat. No matter how good her team managed to get at the cup stacking, she wasn't sure they could match the Muffin Mansion for pure spectacle.

They finished the routine with a flourish, and the only one who was off was Roger. Gib lit into him, and Candace couldn't help but feel sorry for him.

"What's your problem, galley rat? Not paying attention? Too tired? Look around, we're all tired. You have to learn to focus."

"Sorry," Roger said dejectedly.

Gib just rolled his eyes.

Becca turned her back on both of them and joined Candace. "Ready for food?"

"Yup."

"In Zone or out?"

Candace hesitated. She would love to eat in the park, but what she wanted to talk about required a little more privacy. "Out."

"Cool."

They ended up at Rigatoni's, one of Candace's favorite restaurants. They ordered and then settled in.

"So, what's up?" Becca asked.

"Well, you are the Zone guru," Candace said.

"I think it's hilarious that's what you think I am," Becca said with a smile.

"You always seem to have good answers."

"What do you need an answer about today?"

"I'm still feeling unsettled about the whole Kurt thing. Part of me wants closure, part of me wants to get back together, part of me never wants to see him again."

"All normal reactions."

"Which one do I listen to?"

"That depends on your specific situation."

"Okay, specifically me," Candace said.

Becca sighed. "You know how I told you fall was a season of change?"

"Yeah."

"Let me tell you about spring."

"What, it's a time of renewal?" Candace asked.

"It can be, but generally speaking it's really a time of new beginnings."

"As in 'old things are passed away; behold all things are become new'?" Candace asked, quoting the Bible.

"Exactly!"

"So, like what? A new beginning with Kurt? I don't know if that's even an option."

"More like a new beginning *without* Kurt."

Candace just stared at her. "I don't understand," she said finally.

"You know for a smart girl you can be pretty dense. Kurt's not the only guy at The Zone who likes you."

Candace flushed. "What do you mean?"

"If you don't already know, I'm not going to spoil the surprise for you," Becca said.

"So what are you saying?"

"I'm saying that I just think it's time to take your life in a new, better direction. Kurt wasn't a keeper, not for you."

"But why?" Candace asked, frustrated.

"Because you want very different things out of life. That is never going to change, no matter how much you wish it would."

Becca was right, and Candace knew it. It was the thing she had always feared about the relationship. She kicked herself for not having listened to herself sooner.

They ate dinner and talked about guys and work. When they were done eating, Candace glanced at her watch. "Uh-oh, I'm going to be late," she said.

"Date?" Becca said, raising an eyebrow. "In which case, why are you having dinner with me?"

"Practice," Candace explained.

"Isn't it late?"

"It was the only time this week we all had free."

"Well, then get going."

"Thanks," Candace said, handing Becca money for her part of dinner. "For everything."

Becca waved her hand. "Thank me by having a great practice. It's going to be embarrassing if no team poses any kind of threat to us," she said, smirking.

Candace did her best to imitate Becca's smirk. "Don't worry, we're a threat."

"To ourselves and others," she added under her breath as she dashed out the door.

Twenty minutes later Candace was back in Sue's dining room, nervously fidgeting with her stack of cups.

They practiced for an hour. It was hard, frustrating work, but Candace was gratified to see that they were making progress. They all agreed at the end to start trying to interlink their designs the next week.

"Don't forget to wear green tomorrow," Sue reminded as they all headed out.

"Green?" Candace asked, drawing a complete blank as to what she could possibly be talking about.

"Saint Patrick's Day," Sue said.

"Oh, my! I practically forgot," Candace said.

"Trust me, I can't forget. If I let my little brother and sister go to school without green, they'll come back black and blue."

"Can't have that."

"Uh, no."

"What about dress code?" Candace asked.

"You mean, you didn't pick up a green striped shirt from costuming?" Pete asked.

"No, should I have?"

"Yeah," Traci said.

"Look, how is it you all know these things and I don't?"

"Candace, you really need to get on the employee website," Sue said.

"Fine, but what do I do for tomorrow?"

"Wear a plain green shirt if you have it," Corinne suggested.

"Or a large green brooch," Pete added.

"I don't own a brooch, green or otherwise."

"You could always go with green socks," Sue said.

"If I got there early, would costuming still have some left?" Candace asked.

Her teammates blinked at her.

"You know, they just might," Pete said at last.

"I didn't even think of that," Corinne admitted.

Candace rolled her eyes.

It was after ten when she made it home. She knew she should go to bed but she was still too keyed up. She sat down at her computer and IMd Josh.

You awake?

Yup. Guess U R 2.

Ya. So … green costume shirts tomorrow?

Good, U heard.

15 min ago.

Oh.

Yeah.

You can probably still get one tomorrow.

Hope so. So, what is the ref website?

www.thezonethemepark.com

Candace clicked on the link and the park's website came up.

Isn't this just the generic site?

Yeah, but look for a little picture of an umpire at the bottom.

Found it.

Click on him.

Candace did as instructed and it took her to a page titled *Referee News and Updates*. The whole thing was jam-packed with information and featured a huge banner across the top that said "Don't forget to get your Irish on!"

Wow.

Yup. Now you know.

Wish I'd known sooner.

Sorry.

So, how are those rehearsals going? Any problems?

Ha ha. Not telling U what R talent is.

Pretty please.

Not even for sugar on top.

Meanie.

A new IM window suddenly popped open. Candace stared at it for a moment in surprise. She fired off a quick message to Josh.

Kurt wants to talk. Fill U in l8r.
Good luck.

She switched back to Kurt's window and the sentence that was making her shake:

Can we talk?

OK, she typed.

I'm sorry.
4 what?
U no.
Tell me.
Breaking up.
In IHOP?
Anywhere.
Oh.

Candace could feel her heart pounding. What was Kurt trying to say? Her mouth was dry, and she couldn't help but think of the conversation with Becca. What if Kurt wanted to get back together? Would that be the wrong thing to do?

Wanna get back together?

Maybe, she typed. It was a lame answer but it was the best way to draw out the conversation and give her time to think, and maybe get some answers from him.

Why maybe?

Why back together?

Miss U.

Miss U 2.

Then why maybe?

We want different things out of life.

So?

That makes things complicated.

Complicated isn't necessarily bad.

No, but it's … complicated.

Candace stared at the screen, frustrated. This would be easier if they could talk face-to-face or at least over the phone. The texting was a buffer, though, for both of them. *We probably need it,* she thought.

Do you love me?

She jumped as she read his text. When they had been dating neither of them had even mentioned the *L* word to each other. Now he wanted her to answer without first declaring for himself. That had to be cheating.

I care for you, she typed.

Not the same thing.

No, it's not.

So, you don't love me?

No, do you love me?

I don't know. Not sure what love is.

At least that's honest.

{shrugs}

So what's the point?

I don't know … but I'd like to try again.

A sudden suspicion filled her.

Is this about your sister getting married?

No. Why?

You dumped me 10 min after telling me she was getting married. Now the wedding's getting close and u wanna make up.

Forget it.

No . . . U started this.

There was no reply. Candace waited for a full minute before asking the question she really wanted the answer to.

Why did U break up with me?

I can't be the guy you want. I've tried, but I can't.

I'm sorry.

Me 2.

Kurt signed out, and Candace just stared at the screen. This was what closure felt like, and it felt rotten. She closed the window and saw the conversation she'd been having with Josh. His status indicated he was still on line.

Still there?

Always. U OK?

I think it's over over with Kurt.

Sorry or congratulations?

Both, I think.

Then consider yourself commiserated with and congratulated.

Will do.

Need me 2 come over?

Yes, but I should go 2 bed instead.

Cool enough. C U tomorrow.

Hasta.

Ciao.

8

Candace arrived at The Zone and stared at the sea of green that greeted her. All the referees were wearing green shirts. Most of the players wore green as well. In case anyone didn't have enough green, the shops sold green T-shirts, green baseball hats, plastic hats, and shamrock jewelry and buttons galore.

Mascots dressed as leprechauns handed out gold-colored coins. The coins could be used to buy things throughout the park. In order to get one, players had to solve a riddle posed to them by a leprechaun.

She made it to the costume warehouse and managed to snag a shirt. She was wearing a green tank top just in case. The last thing she wanted was to be pinched on her way to the costume warehouse.

Wearing an official green-striped ref shirt, she stowed her stuff in the Locker Room and headed for the Candy Counter. She slowed as she approached. Standing in front of the door, arms crossed over her chest, was Lisa.

Candace briefly considered trying to slip past, but there was no way the other girl wasn't waiting for her. Candace took a deep breath and halted three feet away.

"Hello, Lisa."

"Candace."

"What do you want?"

"I want you out of my way."

"From where I'm standing, you're the one blocking the entrance."

"I'm talking about Kurt," Lisa said, eyes blazing.

"Look, Kurt and I have broken up. What more could you possibly want?"

"Your head on a silver platter."

"Sorry to disappoint you, but I'm not John the Baptist."

"What?"

"Never mind," Candace muttered. "Look, it's over, he's free. Have at him."

"He's still in love with you."

"No, he's not," Candace fumed. "And even if he were, that wouldn't be my fault. Maybe instead of spending all your energy harassing me, you should spend a little bit on trying to win him over."

She stepped forward, every muscle tensed, and for a moment Candace thought Lisa was going to hit her.

"Ladies, violence is never the answer," Josh said, interposing himself smoothly between them.

"What are you, her keeper?" Lisa asked.

It was uncanny how many times Josh seemed to come to her rescue. Candace wondered if he had somehow managed to tag her with a GPS sensor.

"Technically no, I'm my brother's keeper. And let me tell you, that's a job," Josh joked.

For one terrible moment Candace thought Lisa was going to hit Josh instead. Her own fists curled at her side. *Turn the other cheek*, she urged herself, even as she realized that if Lisa laid a hand on Josh she would drop kick her into the next Zone.

"This isn't over," Lisa hissed.

"But it should be," Candace said, doing her best to keep her voice even. "Seriously, the only one standing in your way is you."

Lisa turned bright red and then turned and stalked away.

"Thanks, Josh."

"It's okay. Try not to let her bug you. I know she's a pain and she makes you miserable, but imagine how she must make herself feel."

"You're right. I wouldn't want to be in her twisted, angry shoes."

Josh chuckled. "I'm sorry, I like that. Angry shoes. Quite an image."

Candace smiled. "Thought you'd like that."

Candace went inside the Candy Counter and was soon up to her elbows in green candies and pastries. A pastry bag filled with green icing exploded in her hands, and she was still covered in it when a group of leprechauns entered the store.

"Top of the morning to you," one of the leprechauns said.

"But it's afternoon," Candace said.

"Top of the afternoon doesn't sound as good," another leprechaun pointed out.

"We could try top of the evening," a third said.

The whole thing would have been hysterically funny if Candace hadn't had a pounding headache.

"Sorry guys, I'm having a bad day," she said.

"We can make it brighter," the first one assured her.

"You know the history of leprechauns, right?" the second asked.

"I can't say that I do," Candace answered.

"Ah, leprechauns are tricksters."

"Really. And we have a wonderful trick for you."

"What?" Candace asked, taking a step back.

The third leprechaun handed her a small cylindrical bit of metal. "We promised Lisa that we would deliver this to you, a gift from her to you."

"What is it?" Candace asked as she took it from them.

The first two shrugged, tipped their hats, and left the store. The third one hesitated. "I don't know for sure," he admitted, dropping the Irish accent. "But it looks to me like a stem cap for the air tube on a tire."

Candace felt sick in the pit of her stomach. She looked at it more closely. It did look like that.

"She better not have hurt my parents' car," Candace whispered through clenched teeth.

"Do you want to send a message back?"

Did she ever. She was pretty sure if she did, though, she would get fired. "No message," she said.

As soon as her break arrived Candace headed for the parking lot. Sure enough, the left front tire was completely flat and missing its stem cap. She heard someone walking nearby and she turned to ask for help.

Her heart sank when she realized it was Kurt. He looked at her in surprise.

"Do you need help?" he asked, eyes moving from her to the tire.

"Yes, please."

"I've got a compressor in my car, I'll get it," Kurt said.

Candace nodded.

He was back in a minute, and soon the tire was filling with air.

"Did you run over anything?" he asked.

"No, but I have a pretty good idea what happened," Candace said grimly as she handed him the stem cap.

"Do I want to know?"

"Probably not, but you deserve to know. Lisa did it."

"Lisa. Why?"

"She blames me for the fact that the two of you aren't a couple."

"But that has nothing to do with you."

"So I've tried telling her. Somehow, though, even though we broke up, I am apparently standing in her way."

Kurt's face darkened. "I'll have a talk with her," he said.

"Thank you."

Kurt finished inflating the tire, replaced the stem cap, and stood up. "So, have you reconsidered what we were talking about last night?" he asked.

She swallowed. He was standing less than a foot from her and pinning her with his magnetic eyes. She was still attracted to him, there was no denying it. For just a moment she thought about closing her eyes and kissing him. It would be easy. *But six months down the road we'd be right back here.*

"Can you look me in the eyes and tell me that you and I will ever be right together?" she asked.

He stared deep into her eyes, looked like he was about to say something, and then turned his head away. "No," he whispered.

"Then I think it's time we stop trying to pretend for ourselves and each other."

He nodded. "You're right. Well, I guess this is it."

"Yes."

"Thanks, Candace. I'll never forget you."

She felt herself begin to tear up, but she refused to cry in front of him. "Same here."

She thought about hugging him, but it just didn't feel right. She wasn't sure they would ever really be friends. They had never been on that path, and something told her they never would.

The irony was that they had been dating for almost a year, and she felt like she hardly knew him. There had been instant attraction between them, but not much else. She hadn't even realized he'd had a sister until a few days before. She wondered if he knew any more about her than she did about him. They were a couple of strangers who fell for each other but remained strangers until the end.

As she watched him walk across the parking lot, she whispered, "Who was that masked man?"

The next afternoon, Kurt, The Zone, and Lisa seemed worlds away as Candace stood on stage trying to capture the spirit of Aldonza.

"Better, now take it from the beginning and remember to project your voices," Mr. Bailey instructed.

Keith, who was playing Don Quixote, groaned. Next to him, Reed, playing sidekick Poncho, made a face. For once Candace smiled at Mr. Bailey's direction. She might have trouble with blocking, emoting, and remembering her lines, but she had no trouble projecting. She could bounce her voice off the back wall of the auditorium. It was an unexpected and happy result of her extensive practice with screaming at the top of her lungs. She and Tamara had played a screaming game as children that had come in handy during The Zone's Halloween events. Tamara didn't have any problem projecting her voice either. Compared to the two of them, it was as though everyone else in the play was whispering.

"How do you do that so well?" Keith asked.

"You have to speak from your gut instead of your throat," Candace said. "It's like putting more force behind the words, but not shouting. The goal is to make the person in the back of the room hear you."

"I'll never get it," Reed said.

"Sure you will. Probably about five minutes before the curtain goes up opening night," Candace teased.

"You're in a good mood," Keith noted as they took their places for the beginning of the scene.

"I'm actually kinda enjoying this," Candace admitted. No one could be more surprised than her by that. She was starting to get more comfortable with the play. It helped tremendously when she started looking at the deeper meaning of the stories, the characters, and their motivations.

On the surface, *Man of La Mancha* seemed like a story about a crazy guy who lived in a fantasy world. The story was a lot more intense than that, though. It was about knowing who you were, personal integrity, and fighting to improve the world and the lives of those around you. They were all themes that intrigued her.

She was really beginning to relate to Aldonza. On the surface, they had nothing in common. From an emotional standpoint, though, they were both struggling to understand who they were and what they wanted out of life. Don Quixote gave Aldonza the courage to change. She felt like in her life The Zone had done that for her. She was a very different girl than the one who had taken a summer job there. She was getting used to the changes and starting to enjoy them.

Tamara had been right all along. It was better to embrace the spotlight, especially when you seemed to be stuck in it.

Candace closed her eyes and took a deep breath, allowing herself to become Aldonza. She opened her eyes and saw Don Quixote and Pancho instead of Keith and Reed.

"Action!"

They ran the scene again and finished just before the bell rang. "Great job everyone. See you tomorrow," Mr. Bailey said.

Candace hopped off the stage instead of taking the stairs and smiled at Tamara.

"You *are* in a good mood," Tamara confirmed.

"Life is great."

"Good. I like you like this, all up and hyper."

Candace snorted. "I'm not hyper. Hyper is Becca."

"No, *insane* is Becca. She's a dot to hyper."

"Fair enough."

"So, wanna do something tonight?"

"I thought you had plans with James?"

"He's got a late meeting," Tamara said, making a face.

"Aw the hazards of dating a businessman," Candace teased.

They headed for Tamara's car. "Every once in a while there's a harsh reminder that he's not a student," she admitted.

"How have your parents been coping with the fact that you're dating an older man?"

Tamara smirked. "Pretty well. They think James is all that."

"Don't you?"

"Of course I do," Tamara said, rolling her eyes. "It just sucks when they gang up on me."

Candace laughed at the image. "Wow, your parents must really like him."

"Love him. I mean, think about it. He's mature, responsible, patriotic, and a Christian. He has a career, and he comes from money, so they know he's not a gold digger. He isn't snooty either, which of course they like. On top of that he's crazy about their daughter and hasn't tried to punch out any of the insane relatives. What's not to love?"

"Well, when you put it like that, I'm surprised your mom isn't picking out china patterns," Candace teased.

"Who says she's not?"

"Are you kidding?" Candace asked as she climbed into Tamara's car.

"No. It's cool, though. James knows I don't want to get married until I'm twenty-one. That gives us three years to date."

"Either that or it gives your mom three years to plan a wedding," Candace said.

"Don't joke. I'm not your average teen. I know what I want out of life, and I know who I am. I love James, and I'm going to marry him. There's no need to rush that."

"You don't think he's going to get tired of waiting?" Candace asked. "After all, he's older, probably ready to settle down."

"Please. If a man really loves you, he'll wait as long as it takes. Look at Jacob in the Bible. He had to work for fourteen years to be able to marry Rachel. Real men don't give up because things are difficult or take time."

It was probably one of the most profound things she had ever heard Tamara say, and she was quiet a minute as she thought about it.

"Earth to Candace, you still with me?" Tamara asked finally.

"No, I'm here. Just thinking, that's all."

"Cool, while you're thinking, tell me where we should go tonight."

"Let's go to The Zone. I haven't eaten dinner there in months," Candace said.

"Okay. I think you're crazy for wanting to go to work on your downtime, but who am I to complain? Besides, I've been meaning to get my season ticket holder trading card."

"I've seen it. It looks good."

"What, do they use the same picture as they do for the ID?"

"Yeah."

Tamara rolled her eyes. "I had hat hair that day. Surely we can do better than that."

Candace grinned. She was sure, for Tamara, they could.

9

When she got home, her parents were both in the living room talking. Her mom jumped up as soon as Candace walked in. She grabbed an envelope off the coffee table and walked toward Candace.

"What is it?" Candace asked.

"Florida Coast," her dad said as her mom handed her the manila envelope.

"A rejection letter wouldn't be so thick," Candace said.

"That's what we were thinking," her mom said, a little breathlessly.

Candace sat down. She realized she was a lot more nervous than she had been opening the UCLA letter. "I'm not sure if I can open it," she said shakily.

"You can do it," her dad said, his voice tight.

Candace felt like she was standing on a precipice. She flipped the envelope over, took a deep breath, and tore it open. Several pieces of paper and a couple of pamphlets spilled out. Candace snatched at the top sheet.

It took a moment before she was able to read it clearly. "I got in," she whispered.

She glanced up at her parents who were holding hands. "What am I going to do?"

Her parents looked at each other, and then her father cleared his throat. "You're going to have to make a decision. However, if I were in your shoes, I'd choose Florida."

Fear washed over her. She had never been to Florida. All her family and friends were in California.

"I'd be all alone," she said.

"It would be okay. We'd be only a five-hour plane flight away," her mom said, trying to sound encouraging.

"And you know, with traffic, it can sometimes take more than five hours to drive from here to UCLA," her dad said, his voice upbeat.

"And you could come home for breaks or whenever you felt like it," her mom added.

"Think of it as an adventure," her dad said.

She felt dizzy. She was excited and terrified all at the same time. *Just breathe*, she reminded herself. "I have to think about it," she said.

"Of course, honey," her dad said.

"No need to rush," her mom chimed in.

She hugged her parents.

"Why don't you call and tell Josh," her mom suggested.

"That's a good idea. I'm not quite ready to tell Tamara," Candace said.

Her parents nodded sympathetically. She climbed the stairs to her room and called Josh. "Hey, I heard a vicious rumor that two girls ran amok at the park tonight and that only one of them is dating my brother," he joked.

She wanted to laugh and tease him back, but she couldn't bring herself to do it.

"Candace, you okay?" he asked after a second.

"I got my letter from Florida Coast," she told him.

"And?"

"I got in."

There was a pause and then Josh gave a victory shout. Candace yanked the phone away from her ear.

"Awesome!" he finally said.

"Thanks."

"Why aren't you shouting?" he asked.

"I'm not sure what I'm going to do."

"Okay, do you want me to help you make a decision, or do you just want me to commiserate?" he asked.

"Commiserate."

"Fair enough. It's a touch choice, Candace, and we can discuss the pros and cons later. Right now, though, look on the bright side. You've got options. Some kids are getting rejection letters, but not you."

"That's true," she said.

"You should take the letters to school and rub them in the nose of that guidance counselor."

Candace smiled. "I guess I did show him," she said.

"I'll say! This is exciting. Either way you're going to have fun, meet new people, and prepare for the future. UCLA or Florida Coast. Lots of people would kill to have that decision."

"I can always count on you to put things in perspective," she said.

"That's what I'm here for. Well, that and to convince you that Florida Coast is the right choice."

She rolled her eyes. "No decision-making today."

"No, I know, just clarifying my position."

"I think your position is already crystal clear."

"Is it?" he asked, with a sudden intensity in his voice that caught her off guard.

"I mean, I know you want me to go to Florida," Candace said, trying not to stammer.

There was silence for a moment. When Josh spoke again his voice was more relaxed. "Totally. It's time to shake up Zone World, and I think you're just the girl to do it."

"I appreciate the vote of confidence."

"What can I say?" he teased. "It's a no-brainer."

The next day at the Candy Counter, she mostly worked at the cash register, but they also let her help make the candied and caramel apples. She hoped to work her way up to fudge by Easter. She also wanted to make the decorated candy eggs that the shop sold.

At least the work was a good distraction from thinking about the future. She still hadn't told Tamara about getting accepted to Florida Coast. She knew Tamara wasn't going to be happy about it, and Candace didn't want to talk to her until she made a decision about it.

Around her, other refs worked and chatted; they were far more experienced in what they were doing. She remembered her first several days as a cotton candy operator. She couldn't make a neat cone, and she ended up with sticky sugary stuff everywhere. At least the apples were a little more containable, even if the toppings were not.

She had just finished a batch of candy apples when Traci appeared with a tray filled with fudge and still more candy apples.

"Candace, can you run this tray out to the cart in the Kids Zone?" Traci asked.

"Sure," Candace said, taking the tray from her. Suspicion suddenly filled her. "I just take it there, right?"

"That's it."

"I don't have to stay there and sell it?"

"No, one of the cart vendors does that. We just have to make sure they have treats to sell," Traci said, looking at Candace like she was paranoid.

Maybe she was paranoid, but she had earned her place at the store and off cart duty. She didn't plan on going back. She took the tray and headed for the Kids Zone. Fortunately, there weren't very many players around, so she didn't worry about being bumped and jostled.

She found the cart quickly and handed the vendor her tray of goodies.

"Thanks, I was starting to run low," the girl said, eyes wide. "Listen, could you do me a huge favor?"

"What is it?" Candace asked. Nearly a year in The Zone had taught her to ask questions first, agree to help second. It was sad, but true.

"I really need to go to the bathroom, but I can't leave the cart. I'm not going to get my break for another hour. I just need three minutes, please."

No! Candace said in her head. Out loud, though, she heard herself say, "Okay, but please hurry."

"I will," the girl promised, racing off.

Candace sighed and took up position behind the cart. She could at least unload the tray she had brought. That finished, she walked around the cart and discovered that it was number five, the one she had spent so much time with in the past.

"We meet again," she said under her breath.

She glanced at her watch. It had been five minutes, and the vendor wasn't back yet. A boy walked up and, after walking around to the front of the cart to look at the price menu, Candace sold him a candy apple.

Seven minutes.

She better not have used this opportunity to take her break, Candace thought. *I can't be out here eight more minutes.*

As the clock ticked, she became more agitated. She sold two more candy apples and a chunk of fudge.

Twelve minutes.

She craned her neck, trying to see if she could spot the other girl coming back. She didn't see her, though.

"What are you looking for?" a little girl asked Candace.

"The girl who works this cart."

"But that's you!"

"No, it's not. I was just giving her a break."

"But you look like you work here," the little girl said.

"I do work here, but over in the Candy Counter in the Home Stretch."

"Then why are you over here?"

"Because I was trying to be nice and help someone out," Candace said.

Fifteen minutes.

The little girl's questions weren't helping any with her own agitation. She glanced at her watch. Even if the other girl had taken her whole break, she was late coming back. Candace reached under the counter for the radio, ready to call for help.

She pressed the intercom. "Hi, this is Candace. I'm over in the Kids Zone babysitting cart five for a minute, and the referee hasn't come back. Please send someone to take care of the cart or have it return to base."

She waited, but there was no answer. After about twenty seconds, she hit the intercom again. "Okay, this is not funny. This is Candace from the Candy Counter, and I need you to send someone to take care of cart five here in the Kids Zone."

Again there was nothing. Candace could feel herself start to panic. "This is so not good," she muttered, as horrific vendor-cart experiences came back to her.

She hit the intercom again. "I cannot be stranded here. I'm due back at my actual job. Someone tell me what's going on."

Again silence. It was possible that the intercom wasn't working for some reason. If that was the case, they might never have heard her calling for help in the first place. Candace did the next logical thing. She hit the red panic button.

Hitting the red panic button was a guarantee that security would descend within fifteen seconds. At least it should have been. It always had. Yet she stood there, and the seconds ticked by with no sign of a security guard anywhere around.

"You have got to be kidding me," she said.

She began looking around wildly. Thanks to the position of the cart she wasn't actually in line of sight of any of the ride referees. In fact she couldn't see a single Zone employee of any kind anywhere.

I have entered the Twilight Zone.

Sooner or later someone would miss her and come looking. Then again, maybe they were swamped at the Candy Counter. Maybe by the time they even realized she was still gone, they would think she was on her dinner break or her shift had ended and she'd gone home. So not cool.

She couldn't count on help showing up any more than she could count on the vendor girl returning. She couldn't just wait it out until the next shift arrived; the girl she relieved could have been on the closing shift. Candace remembered all too well the night she and Kurt had spent trapped inside the theme park when her cart malfunctioned over the summer and no one came to help. She refused to do that again. Last time, she had ended up being part of an urban legend she couldn't get away from. Who knew what could happen this time?

She determined then and there that, when it was all over, she was going to put together a handbook for cart referees and anyone else who might have an encounter with one. No one should have to go through the things that she had gone through. She also briefly considered lobbying for the retirement of cart five, but rationalized that they were probably all just as bad. She took a deep breath and made a decision.

She grabbed a doily from underneath one of the fudge squares and piled the remaining fudge back on the tray that started the whole mess. She picked up a pen and scribbled Out of Order on the doily and propped it in the front window of the cart. Then she punched in a code and removed the cash tray from the register.

She put the fudge tray on top of it and, after a brief internal debate, headed off for the cart parking area. First things first. She would alert the supervisor there to the problem, hand over the cash tray, and then take the food back to the Candy Counter and explain what had happened.

She made her way to the cart parking area without incident. She noticed that she didn't pass a single security guard along the way. When she made it there, a supervisor she didn't know looked at her quizzically over the tops of his glasses.

"Can I help you?" he asked.

"Yes. I'm Candace from the Candy Counter. I'm here to report a problem with cart five over in the Kids Zone."

"What's wrong with it?"

"Well, I brought fudge and candy apples from the Candy Counter to the cart. I agreed to spell the girl working it so she could run to the restroom, and she never came back. I tried the intercom but got no response. I also tried calling security but nothing happened. I grabbed the cash tray. Here you go," she said, handing it over.

"You left the cart unattended?"

"I put an Out of Order sign on it and removed the food. I don't think much is going to happen to it. Now, if you'll excuse me, I've got to get back to the Candy Counter."

She turned and left, walking quickly back toward the front of the park. She burst into the Candy Counter and was surprised to see the referees clustered around Martha. She had a walkie-talkie in one hand and a stopwatch in the other.

"Twenty-five minutes," Martha noted. "Not bad."

10

"What's going on?" Candace asked as she stared at Martha and her coworkers.

"It's called a test," Martha said with a smile. "And I'm pleased to say you passed."

"Twenty-five minutes is an excellent time," Traci said.

"Exactly. Not too fast, not too slow, but just right," Martha said.

"I'm glad to be the baby bear in the Goldilocks story, but would someone tell me what is going on?"

"Sorry, Candace. It's one version of a test we give to prospective management."

"Then why give it to me?"

"It's the final stage of the scholarship competition. Each of the five of you were given a test."

Candace started to panic. "Nobody warned me about that."

"That's kinda the point. Don't worry, you did fine."

"So, what, everything that just happened, you knew?"

"Very good. I knew you'd catch on quick," Martha said with a smile. "Yes, essentially. We arrange for you to be trapped with no support, and we observe how you solve the problem and how long it takes you."

"Did I do the right things?" Candace asked, her mouth suddenly dry.

"Perfection. You gave enough time for the referee to return to the post. Then you tried to get help from a supervisor. Next you tried to alert security to the problem. Finally you resolved it yourself by safeguarding Zone property and players without too much fanfare or fearmongering. I couldn't have done better myself."

"Well, I'm glad to hear that," Candace said, still feeling a bit bewildered.

She handed her trays to one of her coworkers. "Was there anything else I should have done, tried?"

"Nope, you were perfect."

"And my time was good?"

"Right between the goalposts," Martha confirmed.

"So, we survive the interview with John Hanson and then whoever scores highest on this gets the scholarship?"

"Not exactly. The ultimate decision is still up to Mr. Hanson. We do provide him with the test data, though. In all but extreme cases, the two worst performers in the test are knocked out of the running. That's more of a guideline, though, than a rule."

"Great, now I'm really nervous," Candace said.

"Don't worry. You're the last of the five to be tested."

"And?"

"In the top three."

Candace sagged against one of the counters in relief. If she had ever doubted that she wanted to win, she couldn't doubt it any more. She wanted to win badly. She wanted to go to Florida Coast and study to be a ride designer. Most of all, she wanted to ride the Balloon Races. She was glad she'd had no idea, when she came to work, how much had been on the line.

"Okay, this was far more stress than I needed today," she said.

Martha smiled. "Why don't you take your break? Go look at all the new decorations in the Holiday Zone or something. Take a walk, breathe deeply. And remember, you're going to be just fine."

"Thanks, Martha," Candace said.

Candace walked outside and breathed in deeply like Martha had suggested. As she breathed, she noticed how the green that had festooned every inch of the Home Stretch had given way to pinks, yellows, and purples.

She turned and walked toward the Holiday Zone and marveled at what she saw. As if by magic, the Saint Patrick's Day theming had disappeared and been replaced by Easter. Spring had officially come to The Zone, complete with bunny rabbits, Easter eggs, and three giant crosses that presided over the Holiday Zone.

Candace found herself under the three crosses, staring up at them and thinking of their significance. Spring was a time of birth and rebirth, death and resurrection. As much as she loved winter, even Candace found that she was enjoying the lengthening days and the warmth of the sun. She couldn't help but feel, too, that there was something wonderful just around the corner.

After a few minutes, she became aware of someone standing silently next to her under the crosses. She glanced over and saw that it was Josh. His face was lifted upward and his eyes were closed. She thought he was praying, and she turned to look away, not wanting to intrude on something so private.

She tried to pray, but too many thoughts crammed her mind. Over all of them, though, was a sense of thankfulness and profound awe. Stains on the dark wood of the center cross looked almost like blood, and a shiver went up her spine.

"Every year these crosses still amaze me and make me feel so small," Josh said.

"They're wonderful ... and terrible all at the same time," Candace replied.

"Makes most other things seem unimportant, doesn't it?"

"Yeah, it really does," she said. After a moment, she added, "I'll see you later. I've got some things to take care of."

Candace knew what she had to do, but she wasn't sure where to start looking for Lisa. Fortunately, she didn't have to search very long. She found her at the second food cart she came across.

"What is it?" Lisa snapped when Candace stopped in front of her.

"We need to talk," Candace said.

Lisa's eyes narrowed and she set her jaw. "Yeah?"

"Yeah. This feud thing is stupid. No guy is worth us sniping at each other like this. I never meant to steal Kurt from you. I don't think I did. Regardless, I'm sorry that you were hurt. I wish we could put it behind us and be— "

"What, friends?"

"I was thinking more non-enemies," Candace corrected.

"I can live with that," Lisa said after a minute.

"Truce?" Candace asked, extending her hand.

"Truce," Lisa agreed, shaking on it.

"See you," Candace said, turning to go.

"That's it?" Lisa called after her.

"Isn't that enough?" Candace asked.

Lisa smiled at her. "Yeah, I guess it is."

Candace returned to the Candy Counter and spent the next hour up to her elbows in apples. When it was close to the end of her shift, Traci appeared and took a seat next to her.

"Hi, I'm on break. I thought we could chat," Traci said.

"Sure, what's up?"

"I'm terrible at cup stacking, and I don't think I'm going to get better fast enough to help our chances in the talent show. I think the team should cut me loose."

"What? We can't do that," Candace said, taken completely by surprise.

"Sure you can, it'd be easy."

"Not an option. You are our team member. Besides, everyone is supposed to participate in the talent contest."

"There are a couple of people, singers mostly, who are doing solo acts. I can do something like that, and I'll be covered as far as participation goes."

Candace stared at Traci. She was right about one thing, Traci wasn't good with stacking cups. Not that any of them except Corinne were much better. Still, without Traci they could move through the training a lot faster.

"No," Candace said. "We got into this together, and we're going to make it through together. If you really want to quit, I can't force you to be on our team, but if you do, have the courage to admit why you're doing it."

"What do you mean?" Traci asked, face pale.

"If you quit, you're doing it for you, because it's too hard and you're scared. You're not doing it for the team. Actually the opposite is going to happen. If you walk away and we only have four people to do this, we have no chance of winning. We need five in order to make the pyramids work. There's no time to start training with someone new even if someone could be persuaded to join us.

"You're not only going to be hurting us, though, you're also going to be hurting yourself. If you run away when life gets hard, then you'll be running for the rest of your life." Candace could tell Traci was upset and angry, but she felt like she needed to hear the truth.

"It's just a stupid talent show," Traci muttered.

Candace smiled and shook her head. "If there's one thing that I've learned at The Zone, it's that there are no stupid, meaningless activities. Each thing we do is an opportunity to better ourselves, push ourselves to be more, and to have courage. They don't do things like the summer Scavenger Hunt and the Talent Show as idle amusements. They put these things on to give us a chance to come together in a spirit of fellowship and competition and to push ourselves to be more than we thought possible."

Traci began to cry, and Candace wrapped her arms around her. "It's going to be okay. We can get through this together. If you want, you and I can start practicing on breaks and stuff."

Traci nodded but didn't say anything. A slight sound caused Candace to turn her head. She saw Gary, standing silently, just inside the door of the kitchen. He turned and walked outside.

Finally Traci pulled away and wiped at her eyes. "You're off the clock," she noted.

"No big," Candace said.

Traci laughed. "No, it's very big. Thank you. No one's ever explained things to me quite that way before."

Candace shrugged. "I'm glad I was in the right place at the right time to help."

"Me too. I'll start bringing my cups and practicing on breaks tomorrow."

"Great. Maybe soon we'll be able to teach Corinne a trick or two," Candace said.

"I'd like that. Now go home."

"You're sure you're okay?"

"Yes, thank you."

Candace left the store and found Gary waiting outside for her.

"You did a good thing in there," he said.

"How long were you standing there?" she asked.

"I got most of it."

"I'd appreciate it if you would keep it to yourself. I wouldn't want people gossiping about this."

"Of course," he said.

"So, what brings you on field?" Candace asked, changing the subject.

"You."

"Me what?"

"I wanted to watch you at work, get more of a feel for you as a person."

"As a person?" she asked, ignoring for the moment the part where he'd wanted to watch her work.

"Yeah. You see, the legends about you are pretty intense. I just wanted to see what kind of person manages to attract so much attention."

"I don't try to, honest. And if you've heard the one about me being trapped inside the park overnight and chased by a psycho killer, well, it's not true. I was trapped overnight in the park, but there was no psycho killer. I was chased by a saboteur through a maze at Halloween, though."

He laughed. "You know, I knew about you before I met you the other day."

"How?"

"Let's just say the urban legends made their way to Florida and Zone World."

Candace groaned. "And here I hoped that if I got the scholarship and went to Florida Coast I could be a little more anonymous."

"Fat chance of that."

"Of getting the scholarship?"

"Remaining anonymous."

"So, why are you being stalker-like?" she asked.

"I told friends in Florida that I met the famous Candy, and they refused to believe me until I got a picture of us together."

"You're joking," she said, stopping abruptly.

"Yes."

"That's a relief," she said as she started walking again. "So, what's the real reason?"

"As the newly returned former scholarship winner, they've asked me to weigh in with my opinion on the top five candidates for this year."

"Seriously?"

"Yeah."

"Do they always do that?"

"No, this year is kind of special. After all, you're practically a celebrity. If it was a popularity contest, you'd win hands down. They wanted someone from outside who didn't know any of the five candidates personally to make a suggestion."

"So, whoever you pick gets the scholarship?"

"It's a little more complicated than that. My opinion does matter, but it's not the only factor."

"So, how do I stack up?" she asked.

"Pretty well. Afraid I can't say more than that."

"I understand," she sighed.

"Hey, before you head home, you want to ride The Spiral?"

"With the guy who created it? Totally!"

A minute later they were waiting to board the ride.

"So, how did you come up with the idea?" she asked.

"I played football with my dad and brothers when I was a kid, and my dad always drilled into us the importance of a perfect spiral throw. He could make balls do things you wouldn't believe. Then I got a summer job working here and was one of the first people to ride Rim Shot, the one where you feel what it would be like to be a basketball. I thought it was cool, but I was disappointed that there weren't any football-themed rides, especially since John Hanson was a quarterback. I heard about the competition and, voila!, I had my ride."

"That's amazing."

Even more amazing was actually getting to talk to the guy who came up with the ride and then screaming hysterically with him on the ride. When they got off, Candace was so dizzy she was staggering. They exited the ride and then stopped for one final look at it.

"Awesome," she said.

"Thanks. Well, I'll see you around, Candace."

"See you," she answered.

She headed for the Locker Room, grabbed her things, and made her way to the parking lot. On the way she checked messages. She had one from Tamara, but all she could make out was a high-pitched squealing sound. For a moment she thought it was some horrible kind of static until she realized it was actually Tamara making that sound.

"What on earth?"

She called Tamara.

"Hello?"

"I can't understand the message you left on my cell phone," Candace said.

Tamara started shrieking in her ear, and the only thing Candace could make out was "You'll never believe it!"

11

"Calm down, Tam, I can't understand you," Candace urged.

"I won a Zone anniversary prize! I never win anything, but I went through the turnstile, and I won!"

"Congratulations. What did you win?"

"I don't know yet, I'm waiting to hear."

"Tamara, where are you?" Candace asked.

"In the Hall of Fame."

Candace turned around and headed back for the Home Stretch. Once she reached the Hall of Fame, she went inside and found Tamara sitting in a chair with a customer service ref.

Tamara leapt to her feet and threw her arms around Candace. "Guess what I won?"

"You know now?"

"Yes! I won dinner for a group at Boone's."

Boone's was the exclusive, members-only restaurant on top of the fort in the History Zone.

"I actually won something! I never win anything!"

"Congratulations, Tam! What are you going to do with it?"

"I've been thinking maybe a party for my parents for their anniversary."

"That would rock," Candace said. "As long as I'm invited, of course," she joked.

Tamara rolled her eyes. "Of course you are!"

"Seriously, that's awesome."

"I've got a party to plan. You'll help me, right?"

"Totally."

Tamara finished up her paperwork, and they left. "So, what were you doing here anyway?" Candace asked.

"Oh my gosh, I forgot!" Tamara said, grabbing her by the shoulders. "I was coming to surprise you. We're going out to dinner to celebrate."

"Celebrate what?"

"I got my acceptance letter to UCLA!"

Candace squealed and hugged her. "Awesome! Congratulations."

"Thank you."

"So, where are we going to dinner?"

"I was thinking of Aphrodite's."

"Rock on."

"Hey, you know what Mr. Bailey said today about us needing as many people on Saturday to help build sets as we can get?"

"Yeah."

"I was thinking we should ask Josh and James."

"Tam, that's a brilliant idea."

"Thought you'd like it. I'll ask James; you ask Josh."

"I could go ask him now. I think he's still working."

"Cool, go do that, and I'll get us a table at the restaurant."

Candace dashed over to the Splash Zone. She found Josh outside the Kowabunga ride. "Josh, I have something to ask you."

"I already told you, you're just going to have to wait until the contest like everybody else. Our talent is a secret."

"It's not that."

"Oh, then fire away."

"Josh, would you come help my drama class on Saturday? We're building sets and could use all the hands we can get."

He looked at her and smiled. "Is Tamara asking James?"

"That's the plan," Candace admitted. "There'll be free lunch."

"Yes, what an enticement," he said teasingly.

"So, help a girl out?"

"Well, when you put it that way, I can't very well refuse, can I?"

"No."

"Fair enough. We'll be there at nine."

"Thank you!"

She waved and ran toward the History Zone. She arrived just in time to be seated. "Josh is on board."

"Awesome. What's the use of knowing big, strong guys if you can't manipulate them into doing hard labor for you?" Tamara laughed.

"Good point."

As soon as they were seated, Candace spotted a couple at a table across the room. "Tamara, look!"

"Who's Sue eating with?" Tamara asked, twisting around to look.

"That's Checkmark."

"Who?" Tamara asked.

"Mark, you know, your pity date from a couple months ago."

"Mark! How on earth did he meet Sue?"

"He works here now at the Kowabunga ride."

"What? When did that happen?"

Candace bit her lip. "It's been a few weeks, I think."

"Okay, clearly I'm behind on all the news. What else haven't you been telling me?"

"Nothing, I don't think."

"Uh-huh. That's what you say now."

Tamara looked back at the couple. "I think he's holding her hand," she noted.

"Good for them," Candace said. "They're both really nice. I hope it works out for them."

She tried really hard not to think about her last experience in the restaurant, when she had just started dating Kurt. She said a silent prayer that it would work out better for Sue and Mark than it had for them.

The next afternoon Candace walked out of the Candy Counter and headed toward the Cantina. Her stomach rumbled angrily, reminding her that it had been too long since she had last eaten.

"Candace, wait up!"

She turned, wondering who had called out to her. She stiffened as she saw Lisa coming her way, waving her arm.

Candace braced herself as Lisa walked toward her. The truce had been in effect for a few days, but Candace was skeptical about Lisa's intentions to maintain it. The other girl stopped in front of her and just stared for a minute. It was creepy, and Candace was about to say something, anything, to break the silence when Lisa did.

"I want what you have."

"Kurt? Fine you can have him. He's not mine anyway," Candace said, rolling her eyes.

"No, not Kurt, the other thing."

Great, now I have something else she wants, Candace thought. She shook her head. "What thing?"

"I don't know what it is. It makes you seem so alive. It also keeps you from punching my lights out, I think."

Candace didn't know what to say. What was Lisa getting at?

"What do you call that?"

"Umm ... God?" Candace asked, taking a shot in the dark.

"Really? Then that's what I want."

"Are you kidding?" Candace burst out. She winced. It sounded bad even to her.

"No. I've done a lot of mean things to you, more than you know, and yet you still try to be nice. I want to know what it's like to be that kind of person."

Candace was instantly concerned about what those other mean things she didn't know about might be. She forced herself to take a deep breath, though, and focus on the rest of what Lisa had been saying. She glanced at her watch.

"I've got a break now. Why don't we go talk?" she suggested.

Lisa nodded and then followed her off field. They found a bench and sat down.

"What do you want to know about God?" Candace asked, not sure how else to start.

"Everything."

Candace laughed. "No one knows *everything.*"

"Well, tell me what you do know."

"Well, I know that God loves us and wants what's best for us. That's why he sent his Son, Jesus, to die for our sins."

She paused, waiting for Lisa to respond or ask a question or something. The other girl just stared at her. Candace couldn't read her expression. She took a deep breath and plunged on.

Candace spent an hour talking. Lisa just listened. She didn't ask questions or anything, and it made Candace nervous. Finally she wrapped it up, and since Lisa didn't seem to have any questions, she asked one of her own.

"Would you like to maybe come to our youth group this week? I know you'll have questions, and it's a good place to start looking for answers."

Lisa stared at her for a long minute before nodding. "That would be cool. Just tell me when and where."

Candace gave her the time and directions. Deep down she realized she was actually surprised that Lisa had agreed to go. Somehow she hadn't believed Lisa was totally serious about learning about God.

Guess I was about as wrong about her as I could be, Candace thought.

"Thank you," Lisa said, further surprising her. "I appreciate the invitation."

Candace thought about offering her a ride, but couldn't quite bring herself to do that. She still didn't like Lisa, even if they did have an uneasy truce and the other girl was seeking God. *Not very big of me, but nobody's perfect.*

"Can I ask you something?" Candace said.

"What?"

"I was surprised that you nominated me for the scholarship."

Lisa rolled her eyes. "I figured if you won, you'd be as far away from Kurt as you could get."

Candace shook her head. She had half suspected that was the reason, but the truth just seemed sad.

Sweat was rolling down Candace's back. They had graduated from Sue's dining room table to the back patio. Sue, Corinne, and Pete were all sweating just as much as she was. Traci, though, looked cool and calm. She had been practicing at work on all her breaks like Candace had suggested, and now she was better than the rest of them. Each of them had five sets of stacking cups. They were trying to create representations of the pyramids of Giza with them.

Sue and Candace, who were evenly matched in speed, were each building one of the smaller pyramids. In the center, Pete, Corinne, and Traci worked together to construct the largest pyramid. Pete and Corinne constructed the bottom part and left Traci to build the top in a blur of flying hands and cups. They were aiming to finish all three pyramids simultaneously, but they were still a few seconds off.

"Break," Sue croaked finally.

They all collapsed onto the grass. Sue's younger brother and sister, who were acting as their audience, went inside and came back out with ice water for everyone. Candace drank hers down thirstily and then fell backward onto the grass.

"Anyone else need Tylenol?" Pete asked, fishing some out of his pocket.

"Yes," Candace moaned. "I feel like my fingers are going to fall off."

"Are you sure we can't just leave it at the pyramids?" Corinne asked.

"We all agreed. Pyramids, Eiffel Tower, Stonehenge," Sue reminded.

"It will be cooler that way," Traci said.

"If we can still bend our fingers," Pete commented.

"It will look awesome," Candace said.

"Okay, let's take a go at Stonehenge," Corinne said.

With a groan, Candace and the others got up.

"We can do this," Pete said. "Just remind me which part of Stonehenge I'm building."

"I don't even remember which part I'm building," said Sue.

"Maybe we should work on the Eiffel Tower next," Corinne suggested.

"Okay, next time somebody remember the diagram," Candace said.

"What diagram?" Traci asked.

"I thought we made a diagram of this last time," Candace said.

"We talked about making one, but we didn't actually do it," Sue said with a sigh.

"Well, then let's make one this time so we'll have it for next time," Candace said.

"I've got a better idea, ditch Stonehenge and pick a new third thing," Pete said.

"Like what?" Traci asked.

No one could think of anything else. Sue went inside and came back out with a large piece of construction paper and some markers. "Fine, but let's diagram it out."

12

Saturday morning, Tamara picked up Candace, and they drove to school where they met up with Mr. Bailey and the rest of the drama class in the auditorium. Mr. Bailey had brought donuts, and Candace eagerly scarfed one down, having overslept her alarm and missed breakfast.

"Okay everyone, today is the beginning of the end. Today we construct sets, which means the play is just around the corner. From here on out, we'll be working harder, practicing longer, and getting used to our sets, props, costumes, and, ultimately, makeup."

The guys in the class groaned at the mention of makeup, and the girls laughed.

"Thank you all for coming out this morning. Thank you also for those of you who have persuaded loved ones to be here."

A couple of fathers nodded tiredly.

"All right, let's get to work," Mr. Bailey said, rubbing his hands together like a villain in some old melodrama.

Candace and Tamara set to work painting some of the walls for the prison backdrop. It was slow going, but they had an easier time of it than some of the others who were working on hinging walls together.

Josh and James showed up at nine a.m., as promised, and were instantly surrounded by admiring classmates of Candace and Tamara.

"My guy," Tamara announced, laying a kiss on James.

Candace laughed at Tamara's marking of her territory. She moved over and hugged Josh, fighting the sudden urge to kiss him on the cheek.

"Thanks for coming," she said.

"Not a problem, because you know we guys have nothing better to do on a Saturday than build stuff," he teased.

"That's why we girls will always need you."

"Well, I guess that works."

"So, what do you want us to do?" James asked.

"Set construction," Mr. Bailey said as he walked up to them. "Glad to see you guys."

"Give me a hammer," Josh said.

"Give me a paintbrush," James chimed in.

"How about I give you both hammers and then graduate you both to paintbrushes later?" Mr. Bailey suggested.

"That works," Josh said.

They all moved toward the stage where several people were already busy hammering. They worked for three hours. Tamara frequently took a break to run over and give James a thank-you kiss. Candace couldn't help but feel a bit jealous. She had the feeling, though, that even if they had still been together, Kurt wouldn't have offered to help out.

Candace finished the section she was working on and moved on to a new part of the wall. Next to her another girl was already busy with her paintbrush.

"Your boyfriend is awesome," Kira said. "So cute and funny, and he's willing to help. Where do I get one like that?"

"He's not my boyfriend; we're just good friends," Candace said.

"Oh. Does he have a girlfriend?"

"No."

"So, he's free?"

"I guess," Candace said, becoming intensely uncomfortable with the questions. Kira was nice, but Candace didn't want her hitting on Josh.

"So, what are you, an idiot?" Kira asked.

"Excuse me?" Candace asked.

"He likes you. You like him. What's the problem?"

"I told you, we're just friends."

"Then you're both idiots," Kira snorted.

Before Candace could retort, Mr. Bailey clapped his hands to get everyone's attention. "Lunch break. Grab a hot dog and a soda," he said, waving to a table at the back of the auditorium.

"Awesome, I haven't had a Casper dog in a couple of years," James said, jogging past Candace on his way to the table.

"Craft services at its finest," Josh joked as he walked up to Candace.

Kira elbowed Candace before taking off.

"What was that about?" Josh asked.

"Just horsing around," Candace said vaguely.

A minute later, Josh, James, Tamara, and Candace had their food and a spot on the floor.

"So, when do we get to see this spectacle?" James asked.

"Two weeks," Tamara said.

"Awesome, we'll be here," Josh said.

"Oh, no," Candace protested.

"What?" Josh asked.

"I don't need you to watch me make an idiot out of myself."

"Come on, Candace, you're going to be great. You already are," Tamara said.

Candace rolled her eyes. "I wouldn't say that. I'm trying, though, and at least I feel like I am starting to understand Aldonza."

"See, you're light-years ahead of me. I don't understand my character much at all," Tamara said.

"You'll figure it out," Candace said. "It's kinda cool when you start understanding who these people are and why they do the things they do."

"Thinking of becoming a professional actress?" James asked.

"No! I don't want people to come to this; I can't imagine if this was my job."

"You're going to be great," Josh said, giving her his most dazzling smile. "And you can't stop me from coming."

"Me either," James chimed in. "Although to be fair, I'm going to be paying a lot more attention to Tamara than you. No offense."

"None taken," Candace said with a laugh.

Candace finally made it home, exhausted and paint streaked. It had been a grueling day, but all the major set work was done. The touch-up work could be done during class time by students waiting for their scenes. James and Josh had stuck in to the very end.

She walked into the kitchen, wanting to get a drink of water before hopping into the shower. Her parents looked up from the kitchen table, their faces serious. Fear pricked her spine.

"What's wrong?" she asked.

"Aunt Bess is sick," her mom said.

Aunt Bess was her dad's younger sister. She lived in Florida, and although they talked all the time on the phone, they rarely got to see her in person.

"What's wrong with her?" Candace asked, fingers curling around the back of a kitchen chair.

"She's going to have a hysterectomy," her father said, his voice shaking slightly.

"Will she be okay?"

"She should be," her mom said.

"When?"

"Friday," her mom said.

"Good Friday?"

"Yes."

"Dad and I are going to fly out for about ten days and help take care of the kids. Uncle Tom's going to have his hands full with taking care of her."

Candace's cousins were six, eight, and nine years old. She had only met them a couple of times. She said a quick prayer for them. They had to be terrified by what was going on.

"We've talked about it, and we don't want to take you out of school," her dad said.

"So, I'm staying here?"

"Yes, I'm so sorry," her mom said.

"It'll be okay."

"We hate the thought of leaving you alone for Easter," her dad said.

"I know Tamara and her family are going to be out of town visiting her grandparents," her mom said.

"It will be okay," Candace said. "I'll find something to do. I'm a lot more concerned about Aunt Bess."

Her mom stood up and hugged her hard, which scared Candace a little bit. "Thank you," she whispered, and her voice was shaking. Candace hugged her back.

Candace finally went upstairs, showered, and then settled into her room. She called Tamara and left a message for her. Then she called Josh and told him about her aunt.

"That's terrible. I'll be praying for her, for all of you," he assured her.

"Thanks, I appreciate it. I'm just freaked out a bit. I'm not used to seeing my parents scared like that."

"Understandable."

It was after midnight when they finally hung up.

Sunday night, Candace and Tamara were a few minutes early to youth group and had staked out their favorite couch. "I'm not happy that you're going to be alone on Easter," Tamara said when Candace filled her in.

Candace shrugged. "It will be fine. I'm sure I can find something to do."

"Are you sure you don't want to come with us to Dad's family reunion?" Tamara asked.

Candace rolled her eyes. Three days trapped with Tamara's extended family was not her idea of a good time. Nor Tamara's for that matter. "I went to one of those like six years ago, remember?"

"How can I forget?" Tamara asked gloomily.

"You could bail and stay with me," Candace suggested.

"Can't. 'Rents are firm about this one," Tamara said.

People were trickling in. Jen came over and sat near them. Suddenly Candace saw a familiar face come in the back.

"She actually showed!" Candace said.

"Who?" Tamara asked.

"Lisa."

"Lisa? The one we hate?" Tamara asked.

"Yes. I mean, no, we don't hate her."

"We don't? When did this happen?"

"I don't know. The last few days. We called a truce, and then she started asking me about God."

"Freaky."

"Tell me about it. Now she's here. Freakier."

Candace waved, and Lisa walked over slowly. Her eyes were wide, and she was staring at everything and everyone. Candace stood up. "I'm glad you could make it."

Lisa nodded, looking distinctly uncomfortable. "Thanks for inviting me," she said.

"Do you want to sit with us?" Candace asked.

Lisa shook her head slowly. "I'm just going to sit in the back."

"Oh, okay, that's cool. Do you want me to introduce you to anybody?"

"No."

Lisa turned and walked toward the back of the room, where she found a seat in the corner. Candace continued to stand awkwardly for a minute before reclaiming her seat.

Candace couldn't help but feel nervous throughout the evening, and she kept glancing back to see how Lisa was doing. The other girl was doing her best to keep to herself despite the efforts of people who were trying to introduce themselves to her. It was a good meeting, and Candace was grateful for that.

When it was over, Candace stood up, but by the time she had reached the back of the room, Lisa had already gone.

"Everything cool?" Tamara asked.

"I guess. I just wish I had a chance to talk to her afterward," Candace said, actually regretting not having offered to give her a ride in the first place.

"Chill. If she wants to talk to you, she will."

"I guess you're right."

Monday afternoon, Candace tried to find Lisa, but she didn't seem to be at work. She finally wandered over and stood under the crosses in the Holiday Zone again, reflecting and praying. Josh found her, and she could tell at a glance that he had something on his mind.

"I have a totally awesome idea," Josh said.

"What?"

"You should spend Easter with my family."

"Really?"

"Yeah. You could come for the whole weekend. It would be fun."

"Your parents wouldn't mind?"

"I already asked them, and they're excited about it."

"That would be great, but, my parents are going to want to know stuff about your family."

"Like what?"

"They're going to want contact information, I'm sure. Phone number, address, *names*."

"Oh." Josh sighed. "I see where you're going with this. You know what, go ahead and tell them. Your parents are cool. I'm sure they can keep a secret."

"So, it's okay to let my parents know who your parents are?"

"Yeah."

She hugged him. "This is going to be awesome!"

"Told you."

When Candace got home, she found her parents upstairs packing.

"Do you need any help?" she asked.

"I think we have it under control," her dad said.

"I just wish we didn't have to leave you alone for Easter," her mom said.

"Josh invited me to spend the weekend with his family," Candace said, not entirely sure how they would react.

Both her parents looked instantly relieved. They stopped packing and sat down on the bed.

"That's very sweet of him," her mom said.

"I'm not surprised," her dad added.

"We should have them over for dinner when we get home," her mom said.

"We'll need their phone number, just in case," her dad said.

"Mr. and Mrs.... you know, I don't think we've ever heard what Josh's last name is," her mom said.

Candace bit her lip.

"What's wrong, honey?" her dad asked.

"You have to promise not to tell anyone. I'm one of the only people at work who knows who his parents are."

"Are they famous?" her mom asked.

"Are they criminals?" her dad asked simultaneously.
"A bit famous. Not criminals."
"Who are they?" her dad asked.
"John and Lilian Hanson, the owners of The Zone."

13

"I didn't see that one coming," Candace's father admitted.

"Josh's parents own the park?" her mom asked.

"Yes, along with Zone World in Florida," Candace affirmed. "At work, people don't know because he doesn't want to be treated differently."

"I could see where that would be difficult otherwise," her mom said.

"When we invite them over for dinner, we'll have the game night of all game nights," her dad said, a smile lighting his face.

"Josh is on my team," Candace said, staking her claim.

"I call John," her dad said.

Her mom stuck her tongue out at both of them.

"What day are you leaving?" Candace asked.

"Friday afternoon," her mom said. "I still wish there was a way for us to spend Easter together."

"I have an idea about that," Candace said. "It won't be on Easter, but we can still celebrate Easter together."

"We're all ears," her dad said.

"Well, you know King Richard's Feast in the History Zone?"

"How could we forget it? We celebrated several of your birthdays there," her mom said.

"Well, I found out that for this entire week, up to and including Sunday, they have a special Easter event called the Great Carrot Brunch."

"The Great Carrot Brunch?" her dad asked. "Is it hosted by bunnies?"

"I think so," Candace admitted.

"You have Friday off school, right?" her mom asked.

Candace nodded.

"What time is their earliest seating?"

"Ten a.m."

Her parents exchanged quick looks. "Let's do it," her dad said.

"Can you make the reservations, honey?" her mom asked.

"Absolutely."

She went to her room, called, and reserved three seats for the brunch. When that was done she hopped on the computer and IMd Josh.

My parents said I can spend the weekend.

Cool. Did they ask about my parents?

Yes. They won't tell, but now they're planning a game night for all of us after Easter.

LOL! That should be fun.

I called dibs on you. My dad called dibs on your dad.

Should have called my mom. She's a wicked good player.

Mom will be happy.

Always a good thing.

Guess what!

You've decided 2 invite all the refs 2 the play.

No!!!!!!!

I could invite all the refs.

Don't U dare!!!

☹

We're going 2 the Great Carrot Brunch Friday b4 they leave.

☺

Can U pick me up there?

Of course. Have u ever been?

(shaking head no)

It totally rocks!

Just 1 # question?

What?

Will there be carrots?

ROTFLOL!!

Well?

No.

Really?

No.

OK confused now.

Of course there R carrots!

Glad 2 hear it.

OK gotta go now.

Everything OK?

Homework.

Yuck.

Tell me about it.

Later.

TTFN.

Candace signed off. Her phone rang, and for a second she thought it might be Josh again, but it turned out to be Tamara.

"What's up?"

"I've made a decision," Tamara said.

"Yeah?"

"I'm going to throw my parents that anniversary party at Boone's with the prize I won."

"They'll love that," Candace said. "Isn't that a bit short notice, though?"

"The prize people said I could pick any of the next six Wednesday nights because they were holding those open for things like this."

"And their anniversary is like in a week and a half, right?"

"Right. So, I'm thinking the Wednesday after next. We're coming back Monday morning."

"Awesome."

"I want you and your parents to come as well as Josh, James, and their parents, but I know your parents don't know the big secret."

"No longer true."

"What! What happened?"

"Josh invited me to spend Easter weekend at his house and gave me permission to tell my parents who his parents were."

"And you didn't tell me!" Tamara shrieked in her ear.

"Sorry, it all just happened," Candace winced.

"This, this is why I don't want you to go away to college. It's hard enough getting information out of you even when I see you every day."

Candace bit her lip. She needed to tell Tamara she wanted to go to Florida Coast. That discussion could wait, though.

"This all happened literally within the last hour, I just finished talking to my parents," Candace said.

"Okay, fine, I forgive you. This is great, though! Now I can have everyone at my parent's party."

"My parents should be home by then, but there's a chance they won't be," Candace warned.

"Wait a minute, what am I thinking? They're going to be gone for what, a week?"

"Ten days."

"What are you going to do next week when you're not at Josh's house?"

"I hadn't thought about it yet," Candace admitted.

"This is awesome! You can stay over here!"

Candace grinned. "Sounds good to me."

"Okay, back to Josh. You're going to be spending the weekend at his house?"

"Yup."

"Wow, this is huge."

"What do you mean?" Candace asked.

"I think he's totally into you," Tamara said.

Candace could feel herself blushing. "We're just friends."

"Uh-huh. And how's that working out for you?"

Candace was at a loss for words.

"That's what I thought. You totally have to make a move."

"Tamara! I can't do that. It's Easter."

"Excuses, excuses. At least tell me you're giving careful consideration to your wardrobe."

"Maybe."

"That's it. I'm coming over tomorrow night to help you pack."

"I've got work tomorrow."

"I know, I'll be over after. We haven't a moment to lose."

The next day at work Candace couldn't help but think about what Tamara had said. She and Josh were just friends. There was something deep inside her, though, that was trying to tell her differently. She wasn't ready to deal with that.

"Hey, Candace," Traci said, waving her hand in front of her eyes.

Candace blinked. "Sorry, what?"

"I was asking if you thought maybe that was a little bit overkill," she said, pointing to the candy apple in Candace's hands.

Candace looked down at it and blushed when she realized she had put more than three times the usual amount of stuff on it.

"Have a little apple flavor with your candy?" Traci joked.

Candace groaned. She tried to fix it, but just ended up making it worse.

"Well, you can either throw it in the trash or give it to Becca," Traci said.

"That's not even funny. Have you seen her on a sugar high? Seriously scary."

"Oh, no, I know."

Candace tossed the apple in the garbage. "What a waste."

"Don't worry about it. Are you okay? You're acting all weird and spacey."

"I guess I've just got a lot on my mind."

"Anything I can help with?"

Candace shook her head. "Not really. I'm pretty sure I have to work this one out on my own."

"Okay, but I'm here if you want to talk. It's break time. I'll be in the storage room stacking cups if you need me."

"Thanks," Candace said with a grin.

After ruining a second apple, Candace got one of the other girls to trade places with her. Thanks to her summer job, she knew she could handle the cash register even in her sleep. Fortunately it was a slow day.

She'd only been in the front a few minutes when Roger came in, his face grim.

"What's wrong?" Candace asked him.

"Talent Show."

"Why? I've seen you guys practice, you're amazing."

He fidgeted and wouldn't meet her eyes. Finally she said, "Can I get you some fudge or a candy apple?"

"No, I came here to talk to you."

"About Talent Show?"

He nodded.

"Then I guess you're going to have to tell me what's wrong."

"No one's ever seen Becca dance."

"What do you mean?" Candace asked. "She's there all the time."

"Directing yes, dancing no. This whole thing hinges on her. Without a star we're nothing more than a glorified chorus line." He sighed and his shoulders slumped further.

"Roger, relax, I'm sure Becca can dance."

"You would think so, but some of us are getting concerned."

"Then why don't you ask her about it?" Candace asked.

"I'm afraid to."

"Okay, why doesn't Gib ask her?"

"I think he's afraid to too."

"So, you're telling me this because . . . ?"

"I'm hoping you can talk to her."

"You're kidding, right?"

"Please?"

"Okay, I guess I can talk to her about it," Candace said.

"Thank you! That would be awesome."

"You know, I'm sure you're all worrying for nothing," Candace said. "I mean, whose idea was it to do the Irish dancing?"

"Becca's."

"See, she wouldn't suggest something that she couldn't do."

"You're probably right."

"I'm definitely right."

"But you'll still ask her?"

"Yes, Roger, relax."

"I'll try."

"So, are you off probation with the Muffin Mansion yet?"

He shook his head. "Not until after Talent Show."

She stared at him for a minute. "Is this why you're stressed out?"

"I'm sure it isn't helping," he said, misery clear in his voice.

She came out from around the counter and gave him a hug. "It's going to be okay, Roger."

"I hope so," he sighed.

Roger left, and Candace went back to the cash register. Five minutes later Becca came through the door. From the look on her face it wasn't a happy coincidence.

"Hi, Becca."

"I know Roger was in here. Spill."

Candace cleared her throat. "He just has some concerns."

"Concerns?" Becca asked, one eyebrow raised.

"Yes."

"About?"

Candace squirmed. This was not the way she wanted to go about having this conversation.

"It's about Talent Show, isn't it?"

Candace nodded.

"And, I'm guessing he's not the only one?"

"No, he's not."

"So, what is it?"

"They're just worried because none of them have seen you dance yet."

"I knew it!" Becca said.

"So, maybe you could just do your part in practice this week just so they can calm down," Candace suggested.

"I can't do that," Becca said.

"Why not?"

"I can do Irish dancing. I had five years of lessons as a kid. That's not a problem. I showed all of them how to do it and they're fine."

"So, what's the problem?"

"In order to dance as fast as I have to and jump as high as I need to for my part, I have to be jacked up on sugar."

"Oh," Candace said.

"So, you see my problem. I was trying to avoid doing my part until the actual Talent Show."

"Well, maybe you can show them what it looks like a bit slower," Candace suggested.

Becca shook her head. "I've tried to do that part slow, without sugar, and I trip over my own feet. If I show them that, they'll panic for sure when there's no need to worry."

"Well, just explain the problem to Gib. He takes such an active role in keeping you away from sugar that I'm sure he'd understand."

"Maybe."

"I think that's your best option."

"Okay, I'll try."

She turned and left, and Candace shook her head. A minute later, Sue walked in.

"Not you too!" Candace said.

"What?" Sue asked, startled.

"Never mind, what's up?"

"I wanted to tell you that I need to push back practice tomorrow night by twenty minutes."

"That's easy. Done. Anything else?"

"No," Sue said, looking at her like she was crazy. "But Candace?"

"Yes?"

"I think you need to relax, you're acting a bit high-strung."

Candace smiled. "Thanks for the tip."

14

When Candace got home, Tamara was already waiting for her in her room. She had strewn half the contents of Candace's closet on every surface she could find. Candace sighed. She wasn't looking forward to putting it all back after Tamara left.

"Well?" Candace asked.

"I've narrowed down your choices to what you see on the bed," Tamara said.

Candace looked closely at her bed. "I see a pair of my jeans and a bunch of your clothes."

"Exactly," Tamara said brightly.

"Tam, as much as I love your clothes, I want to wear my clothes."

"Are you okay?"

"Long, long afternoon," Candace said.

"Wanna talk about it?"

"Not particularly."

"Okay, then let's get you packed."

"That's what I love about you, Tam. There's no stopping you when you make up your mind about something."

"That's true."

"Show me what you're thinking."

It took over an hour, but they finally agreed on several outfits including one just-in-case formal. Tamara opened one of Candace's drawers and tossed a bikini onto the pile of clothes.

"What's that for?" Candace asked.

"I think they have a pool."

"Oh."

Tamara snagged a pair of boots out of the closet. "Do you think they have horses?"

"Tam, change your address; you've officially moved to Fantasyland."

"Can't blame a girl for dreaming."

When they finished, they sat down on Candace's bed and surveyed the damage.

"I think we did well," Tamara said.

"I think I have enough clothes packed for three weekends," Candace sighed.

"You know, if they ask you to stay next week, it would be okay with me," Tamara said. "Don't get me wrong, I'm totally excited that you're spending the week at my house, but I'd understand."

"And something tells me you and your bikini would be putting in a regular appearance," Candace teased.

"You know it."

Candace hesitated. She knew she needed to talk to Tamara about college, but she had been putting it off. She wasn't going to get a better opening, though.

She hugged Tamara. "I'm so grateful to have a best friend who understands," she said.

"Me too," Tamara said.

"We'll be best friends forever, no matter what."

Tamara's eyes narrowed. "You're going to go to Florida Coast, aren't you?"

"I think so," Candace said.

Tamara stood up abruptly, her eyes flashing fire. "Candace, we've been planning UCLA for years. That's the only place I even applied. How could you turn your back on me and go to some school in Florida you never even heard of until a couple of months ago?"

"Because I think it's the right thing to do," Candace said. "Up until a couple months ago I didn't have any ambition, any plans. Now I do."

"So, what, you think I don't have any of those things? Well, I do. I planned to go to UCLA with my best friend. Suddenly that's not good enough? What, you want me to be a doctor or lawyer or something? Kurt wasn't good enough for you and you dumped him. Now you're doing the same thing to me."

Candace had never been so angry at Tamara before. She stood slowly, hands balled into fists. "Knock it off, Tammy!"

Tamara turned completely white and started shaking. "How *dare* you say that to me!" she hissed.

Tammy had been what Tamara's one truly evil relative had called her when she was little, refusing to acknowledge that it wasn't her name. Tamara hated the name with a passion and until that moment Candace would never have dreamed of using it.

"Because you're acting like a spoiled five-year-old, and it's really ticking me off," Candace said, forcing her voice to be cold.

In that moment it seemed like their entire friendship flashed before her eyes, and Candace believed it was the end. It was a stupid thing to throw fifteen years of friendship away on, but there was a line in the sand. She stood her ground and matched Tamara glare for glare. Once upon a time she would have caved, apologized, and backed down. Not anymore. They stared at each other for what seemed like five minutes without saying a word. Then, to her surprise, Tamara crumpled to the floor and buried her face in her hands.

She cried, and Candace let her. She knew that this was as hard on Tamara as it was on her, maybe even more so. Candace was breaking their long-standing plan to go to college together. Tamara must feel left behind.

Finally Tamara looked up; her eye makeup running down her cheeks. "You promise me you'll call every other day?"

"Yes."

"Promise that you'll come home on breaks and I can visit you."

"I promise."

"Promise that I'll always be your best friend no matter what?"

"Always," Candace said, taking a seat next to her on the floor.

Tamara threw her arms around her neck. "Florida isn't going to know what hit it," she sniffled.

"Neither is UCLA," Candace said.

"You're right, we can cause more damage apart," Tamara said, choking on a laugh.

"Absolutely. I'll shake up the East Coast, you shake up the West Coast, and I'll meet you in Texas," Candace said.

"And we'll have barbeque," Tamara said.

"The best in Texas."

The next day, Candace found herself again under the crosses in the Holiday Zone. She didn't know exactly why, but it seemed like they kept calling out to her. She had been a Christian since she was four and had seen dozens of crosses both small and large, but somehow these touched her more deeply.

"Hello," a soft voice said beside her.

She turned to see Lisa standing next to her.

"Hi."

She wasn't sure what else to say so she turned back to the crosses. They stood for a minute in silence before Lisa broke it.

"Thank you for inviting me to your youth group."

"I'm glad you came, although I was sorry that I didn't get a chance to talk with you afterward," Candace said.

"I really wasn't in the mood to talk."

"I get like that sometimes," Candace said.

"I'm jealous of you," Lisa said. "And I don't know how to stop. I've been thinking about it, and no matter how many times I try to hurt you, it never works out that way. I feel like I'm only hurting myself."

"There's really not that much to be jealous of," Candace said.

Lisa laughed, a soft bitter laugh. "I think the sad part is that you really believe that."

"Everything that's happened to me is not that big a deal."

"Don't, please."

"Okay," Candace said. She had no idea how to help Lisa. She was still somewhat amazed that she wanted to help her.

"My parents are not nice people," Lisa said. "I moved out last year on my eighteenth birthday and tried my best to forget my past. I got myself a job and a nice boyfriend who made me feel safe. I managed to trash the relationship, though, and I put my job at risk by taking my anger and frustration out on you.

"You have a good home and parents that care. You waltzed in here and managed to win over everyone here, including Kurt. You got the fame, the praise, and the guy. The worst part was, you didn't even seem to appreciate what you had.

"I'd have given anything to have what you were handed on a silver platter. Life's not fair, though. I learned that before I learned how to walk, and yet it still surprises me sometimes."

"I'm so very sorry," Candace said, not sure what else she could say.

"I spent a lot of time trying to figure out what makes you special. It wasn't looks, or wit, or talent. I finally convinced myself that you weren't special, just incredibly lucky.

"But you *are* special. I've finally begun to see it. The funny part is, it has nothing to do with you and everything to do with what you believe. I hated being at your youth group. Everyone there has had a good life, a decent upbringing, and no understanding of how cruel the world really is. I did like what your pastor said about God, though. That he saw and cared even when no one else did. I want him to see and care about me."

"He already does," Candace said quietly. She pointed to the cross. "That's what this is all about. Jesus sacrificed himself for each one of us."

"No one has ever sacrificed anything for me," Lisa said.

"Yes, someone has, and now you know it."

"I think I know why so many people like to say they don't know if there is a God."

"Why?" Candace asked.

"If they acknowledge that he exists, then the burden is on them to do something about it."

"You know there's a God," Candace said.

"Yes, I can't explain it, but I know he must be real."

"Then what are you going to do about it?"

"I want to be like you."

"All you have to do is ask Jesus into your heart and to forgive you for what you've done."

"I'm afraid," Lisa said.

"Of what?"

"Of losing who I am. If I let God forgive me, does that mean I have to forgive others?"

Candace bit her lip as she struggled to figure out how to answer her.

"No, you don't have to, but ultimately I think you'll want to. It will make your life better. Look at what you said about me. How you felt about me only hurt you. But, no, it's not a requirement of salvation, although it often ends up being something of a side effect."

Lisa nodded. "Will you pray with me?"

"Yes."

Standing there under the cross, they bowed their heads and as Lisa prayed, Candace began to cry.

"Let's take it from the top," Candace said, picking up her stacking cups.

"Stonehenge at quarter speed and in rhythm," Pete said.

"Then the Eiffel Tower at half speed with take down slightly faster," Sue said.

"Last the Pyramids of Giza at full speed with lightning take down," Traci said.

Corinne nodded. "If we can pull this off, it's going to look amazing."

They had finally gotten all three patterns down. Doing it in order and at the right speed was the next challenge. Talent Show was coming up fast, and Candace could tell they were all getting worried. She figured all they needed was to make it through once, and then they wouldn't have to stress until after Easter.

Pete knelt and began to pound out the rhythm for Stonehenge. Then they began. She kept her eye on Sue as she worked. She and Sue were still evenly matched in speed. Sue was slightly better at staying with the rhythm, so watching her helped.

They successfully put Stonehenge up and took it down. Then they launched into the Eiffel Tower. It went up without incident at the correct speed. Take down went even smoother. They paused and then began the pyramid.

The *clack clack clack* of the cups was all she could hear as she built her pyramid. She reached the top, and a surge of joy filled her. They were going to make it! They were going to have a smooth run. She placed her last cup on top of the pyramid and then stared in horror as it wobbled and almost fell. It finally settled, though, and Candace stood up straight with the others and then took it down.

The last cups all hit the ground simultaneously. Candace bounced to her feet, her arms up like an Olympic gymnast who just stuck the landing.

There was silence for a moment, and then very quietly Traci asked, "Did we do it?"

"I think we did," Pete said, sounding dazed.

They began to shout and high-five each other.

"Thank goodness," Sue said. "I didn't have one more in me tonight."

"I don't think any of us did," Corinne said, wiping the sweat from her brow.

"Congratulations to us," Candace said. "We officially know what we're doing."

"Now we just have to practice until we can do it in our sleep," Pete said.

"More like be able to do it with stage fright," Sue said.

"I for one refuse to get that," Traci joked.

"Oh yeah, that's for wimps," Pete said.

"Do we know what our competition looks like?" Candace asked.

"I've heard rumors Muffin Mansion isn't doing so well," Corinne said.

Candace shook her head. "I wouldn't pay attention to those rumors. No matter what you hear, they're still the team to beat. Does anyone know what the Kowabunga team is doing?"

"Not a word," Pete said. "I've never seen a team manage to keep a secret this long."

"I heard some of the Game Zone guys are doing some riff on the games themselves, you know, trick shots with balls, tossing rings over moving objects, that kind of thing," Sue said.

"That will either be totally awesome or completely lame depending on how they do it," Candace said.

The others nodded agreement.

"Do you think we have a chance?" Sue asked.

"There's always a chance," said Pete.

"But a real chance?" Corinne asked.

"I think we have a chance at second," Candace said. "I don't think we'll get first unless something unforeseen happens to the Muffin Mansion team."

"So, they're the team to beat," Traci said.

"Looks like," Pete added. "I figure everyone knows it too."

"I guess they should be watching their backs," Corinne said.

"I think I need some more lemonade," Candace said. "We've got time to practice still, and I think we're going to be great. You'll see."

"How's rehearsal for your play coming?" Pete asked, changing the subject.

Candace smiled wryly. "It seems all I do these days is practice for one thing or another. It's going well, though."

She took a deep breath. "I'd like you all to come," she said.

"That would be great," Traci said.

"I'll be there," Sue said.

"Great, bring your sibs."

"I'd love to come. I've never actually seen a live play," Corinne admitted.

"I'll be there," Pete said, giving her one of his rare smiles.

"Great," Candace said despite the sudden sense of fear that threatened to overwhelm her.

15

When everyone else had left Sue's house, Candace lingered behind. "You can invite Mark to the play too," she said.

Sue blushed. "Thanks."

"He's a nice guy," Candace said.

"He really is. I'm so glad I met him. You know I really need to thank you."

"Me, why?" Candace asked startled.

"He told me that he came to work for The Zone because you made it sound like so much fun. We wouldn't have met if it weren't for you." Sue laughed. "I owe you a lot more than that actually. The scholarship from Tamara's parents, getting everyone to bring Christmas to us, and inspiring Becca to give me the golden candy cane so that we won all those prizes—food, gas, everything we needed, really. I'm not sure where'd I'd be right now if it weren't for you."

Candace felt a lump in her throat. It was funny. It seemed like lately all people were doing was telling her how much she had impacted their lives for the better. It made her feel so humble, because she knew she really hadn't done much. Somehow God had worked through her, though, to touch the lives of others.

I always thought you had to make sacrifices and grand gestures to change people's lives. It seems that sometimes all you actually need to do is show up.

"Thank you," she whispered before hugging Sue. "The truth is all of you have done more for me than you'll ever know."

Soon they were both crying. "You know, I think you're going to do great things for this world."

"Starting with Florida?" Candace asked with a laugh.

"No, starting here. Never be afraid to be who you are."

Candace went home and invited everyone she knew to the school play. After all, she had already started inviting a few, no need to discriminate. She couldn't get out of her head what Sue had said about not being afraid to be who she was. She often felt like a confused, easily embarrassed young woman who was spinning out of control. If she was going to take Sue's words seriously, then she couldn't be afraid to let her friends see just that.

And I'm never likely to be more confused, more embarrassed, or more out of control than I am going to be on that stage, she thought.

Friday morning, Candace woke up more excited than she could ever remember being. She had no idea what to expect out of the weekend, but knowing Josh, she should expect the unexpected. She also couldn't wait to see the Great Carrot Brunch.

They loaded up the trunk with her luggage and her parents' and then drove over to The Zone. They walked to the History Zone and entered the castle.

Candace and her parents followed the waitress into King Richard's, and she was awestruck. She had expected the place to be decorated in the same pastel hues as the rest of the park. Instead, though, they had gone the exact opposite. She felt like she had stepped onto the set of a biblical movie.

"I feel like I'm in ancient Jerusalem," her dad said, mirroring her thoughts.

"I had no idea they did anything like this," her mom marveled.

They were soon seated at their section of one of the long tables that ran nearly the length of the hall. Candace glanced around and was surprised to see how many referees were there with their families. Several saw her and waved, and she waved back.

"What, do you know everyone here?" her dad joked.

"Pretty much," she said. "I don't know all their names, but the faces are familiar."

A few minutes later the room was packed, and the waitresses began serving the food. Every course featured carrot of some sort. There was even carrot soup.

As it turned out, the meal was more of a dinner theater. On the stage at the front of the hall where King Richard normally presided, they presented an Easter play. When they came to the part where Jesus had to carry his cross, the actor shouldered the wood and walked down the aisles between the tables. By the time they came to the crucifixion, she could see a lot of people wiping their eyes, including her dad.

"I think this must be one of the most amazing Easters we've ever had," her mom said.

When the brunch was over, they met Josh in the parking lot, and Candace transferred her bags to his car and hugged her parents.

"Make sure you call," she told them.

"We will," they promised.

"Josh, thank your parents for us," her dad said.

"I will. Happy Easter."

"Happy Easter," her mom said, giving Josh a hug as well.

They finally drove off, and Josh turned to her. "Shall we?"

She nodded.

Fifteen minutes later they were parking in front of Josh's house.

Josh and Candace walked up to his front door. "What's wrong?" he asked.

"I'm nervous," she admitted.

"Why? You've met my parents . . . at least my dad . . . before."

"Yeah, but never as your dad. Just as Mr. Hanson, owner of The Zone," she said.

Josh grinned. "It's okay. He's much cooler as my dad."

Candace smiled back.

John Hanson threw open the door. "Candace, welcome and Happy Easter!"

"Thank you, sir," she said.

"Call me John. Saves me from calling you Miss Thompson."

She nodded. "I can do that."

"Excellent, then we'll get along just fine. Come meet Josh's mom."

It was easy to see the family resemblances. While James was a little more driven, like their father, Josh obviously got his more laid-back personality from Lilian. She hugged Candace when they were introduced.

"I've heard so much about you, it's nice to finally meet," Lilian said.

"It's good to meet you too."

Their house was larger than Tamara's, but it had a different feel to it. Tamara's home was very refined and sophisticated. Josh's house was more fanciful.

"Shall I give you the grand tour?" Josh asked.

Candace nodded.

"Make sure you start with Candace's room, so she can drop off her bags," Lilian said with a smile.

Candace followed Josh up a curving staircase. Portraits that looked like they had been painted during the Renaissance hung majestically on the walls. *Must be Josh's ancestors*, Candace thought, until she spied one portrait in particular.

"What?" Josh asked, noticing that she had stopped.

"This portrait," she said, pointing to one of a young man in period clothing who seemed to be smirking.

"Yes?"

"It's you." She meant to say *looks like you*, but the more she stared at it the more she was certain it was Josh.

"Very good! You'd be amazed how many people never figure that out," he said with a laugh.

She looked at some of the other portraits and was able to identify James, John, and Lilian.

"You guys are crazy!" she said.

"It has been said."

Candace started laughing. "I love it."

"I have a feeling one of these days Tamara's portrait will be up there," Josh said.

"Lucky," Candace responded before she knew what she was saying. Horrified, she gazed up at Josh, but he just shrugged.

"I'm not so sure. I wouldn't want to be married to my brother."

Candace started to laugh again. "Let's hope not!"

They continued up the stairs, and Candace tried to put the portraits out of her mind. At the landing they turned left and walked down a long corridor that looked like something from an old haunted house movie. Heavy wooden doors were shut, hiding the rooms that lay beyond.

At last they stopped at one on the left close to the end of the hallway. "This one's yours," Josh said.

Candace held her breath as he opened the massive wood door. She stepped inside and promptly fell down on the floor laughing. The entire room was decorated like a massive candy store. Giant pillow candy corns decorated the bed. A wind chime made of candy canes swayed in the breeze from the open window. Posters advertising every kind of sugary treat known to man decorated the walls. The rug in front of the bed was shaped like a fluffy cloud of cotton candy, and a bouquet of candy apples was skillfully arranged in a vase on the nightstand.

Josh set her bags down and then joined her on the floor. She wiped the tears from her eyes.

"How did this happen?" she asked.

"We wanted you to feel at home," he said.

"Whose idea was this?" she asked, looking accusingly at him.

He lifted his hands defensively. "Not mine."

"It's gotta be your dad then."

"Nope. This was mom's doing."

"Your mother? That sweet, laid-back woman?"

"Oh, yeah. Most people don't truly get my parents as a couple until they're on the receiving end of something like this. This is all Mom. She has a twisted sense of humor, and don't let that laid-back thing fool you. She's every bit as competitive as Dad."

"I guess she wasn't kidding when she called this my room."

"Nope. Not even a little bit."

"Your family is so weird!"

"I know. Isn't it cool?"

"Yes!"

Candace imagined what a guest room for Tamara might look like, and she laughed until her sides hurt. Finally she struggled to her feet. "I think I'll take the rest of the tour now."

"Absolutely," Josh said as he placed her bags next to the closet. "Plenty of time to unpack later."

He led her back into the hall and to the door directly across from hers. "This is my room," he said.

She followed him inside and smiled. The room was decorated like a surfer's dream. There was surfing art and artifacts everywhere. The room was blue and white, and it definitely left the impression that you were in the ocean. Framed posters for surfing movies decorated the walls.

"Very cool," she said.

He grinned. "And now the rest," he said, leaving the room and heading back toward the stairs.

Downstairs she followed him from living room to kitchen to dining room to two different game rooms. They ended up going down a spiral staircase to the basement where the movie theater was. The screen was huge, and there were thirty real movie theater chairs arranged so that every seat had a great view.

"Wow. Now this rocks."

"Yeah. I've caught Dad watching television down here a few times," Josh said with a smile.

"Can't say that I blame him."

"Me either. Mom would kill him, though. She has a strict rule. The theater is for movies only. She doesn't lay down the law often, but when she does, watch out."

They climbed back up the circular staircase and found Josh's parents in the kitchen.

"Just in time for lunch," John said brightly.

"What are we having?" Josh asked.

"Deviled egg sandwiches," Lilian said.

"Is it just me, or is it wrong to eat devil anything on Good Friday?" Candace joked.

Total silence greeted her. Terrified, she wondered if she had somehow insulted them. She needn't have worried because they finally burst out laughing.

"I can't believe I never thought of that," Lilian said.

"We've been having deviled egg sandwiches on Good Friday as long as I can remember," John said, wiping his eyes on the back of his hand.

"Candace, where have you been all these years? Clearly we need you to save us from ourselves," James said as he walked into the room.

"Hey," Candace said.

"Welcome," he smiled. "Too bad Tam couldn't come, it'd be a regular party."

Candace shrugged. "They're off visiting her grandparents back East."

"I know. I thought about trying to wrangle an invitation, but there will be plenty of time for that later. Besides, apparently in the real world we're expected to work on Spring Break," he finished wryly.

"Stinks to be an adult," John said straight-faced. "Personally I don't recommend it."

It was amazing how in just a few short minutes Candace felt completely at ease with Josh's family. Lilian passed out deviled egg sandwiches to everyone. On a whim Candace broke off a piece of her bread and tossed it at Josh.

It hit him in the middle of the forehead. There was complete silence for a moment, and then John leaped to his feet. "Food fight!"

16

Suddenly the air was filled with deviled egg sandwich missiles. A quarter of Lilian's sandwich landed on Candace's head, and she squealed as it slid down her hair.

"Gross!" She took aim and hurled part of her sandwich toward James who had picked up a chair and was using it as a shield. The sandwich flew apart and splattered against Lilian.

"Shrapnel!" Lilian shouted. "Take cover." She dove under the kitchen table, sliding on some deviled egg on the floor.

When Josh ran out of sandwich, he dove for the loaf of bread and the bowl of egg salad still on the counter. He seized the bread, but his dad beat him to the bowl of egg salad, most of which ended up down Josh's shirt.

Candace shrieked as Josh wadded a piece of bread into a tight little ball and pegged her with it. Before he could launch another, James dropped the chair and dove on top of him. Candace watched as the two brothers wrestled over the bag of bread. When it seemed that Josh was about to win, Lilian swooped in, grabbed the bag, and then scrambled onto the counter where she stood up, holding the bag high.

"I'm the only one left with ammunition!"

"What are your terms for surrender?" John asked.

"The terms are these. Josh and James clean up. John must cook a nice dinner by himself. Candace has to go shopping with me."

"One moment," John said.

James and Josh scrambled over next to him, and he signaled Candace to join them. The four of them huddled up, and the former quarterback took the lead. "Those are some of the best terms she's ever offered."

"I think we can take her," Josh said. "I say fight."

"I agree, but if we try and fail, no telling what she'll demand," James said. "I say surrender."

"Candace, what about you?"

Candace felt like she was having the most bizarre dream ever. Still she did her best to play along. "Shopping doesn't sound bad to me, so I say surrender."

"Two for surrender, one for fight," John mused. He glanced over his shoulder at his wife. "As much as I hate to do it, I have to say surrender. We can't risk a failed siege against her."

They all straightened up, and John turned to Lilian. "We agree to your terms; we surrender."

She broke out into a smile, dropped the loaf of bread onto the counter and hopped onto the floor. "Smart choice."

"That was unreal," Candace said, as she looked around at the mess.

"Work hard, play hard, it's the family motto," John said with a lopsided grin.

Candace started giggling. It was hard to take him seriously while bits of deviled egg were slowly sliding down his cheeks.

"Come on, Candace, let's get cleaned up. We've got some shopping to do," Lilian said. "Have fun, boys," she tossed over her shoulder as she sailed from the room.

Upstairs, Candace discovered that she had her own bathroom that she hadn't noticed earlier. She hopped into the shower, washed all the deviled egg out of her hair, got dressed, and met Lilian at the bottom of the steps twenty minutes later.

"You're fast. Good," Lilian said approvingly.

"Bye-bye, boys," Lilian said as she and Candace moved toward the front door.

"Have fun storming the mall," John said.

"Think they'll be done by the time we get back?" Candace asked.

"It would take a miracle," Lilian said.

The two women turned when they reached the door and in unison said, "Bye-bye."

Lilian's car turned out to be a sleek red Corvette. Candace usually didn't pay too much attention to cars, but she couldn't help but admire Lilian's as she slid into the passenger seat. "Beautiful car."

"Thanks. Do you have a preference which mall?"

Candace shook her head.

"Okay, we'll go to Stoneridge. It's closest."

They pulled out of the driveway and were on their way.

"Are food fights common?" Candace asked.

"I'm sorry. We can be a bit much to handle if you're not used to it," Lilian said.

"No, it was fun, just ... unexpected."

Lilian laughed. "Expect the unexpected, that's what I always say. I'd guess there's a food fight about once a month."

"Wow, and how many of those do you win?"

"A little more than my share. When you live with three guys, especially three big, strong guys, you learn to be smart and fast."

"I guess so. That was awesome."

"I'm glad you were amused. A lot of young women would be heading for the hills right about now," Lilian said. "Don't get me wrong; we have a lot of wonderful friends. Most of them, however, don't spend time with us at home."

"Wow, then I'm really flattered that you're letting me spend the weekend," Candace said.

"It was our pleasure. Josh thinks very highly of you, and so do James and John. They're all very good judges of character. To be honest, I'm glad to have a little time for just us girls so we can get to know each other better."

"Me too," Candace said.

Within a couple of minutes they were at the mall. Lilian pulled a scarf out of the glove compartment and wrapped it around her head.

"I know, it's a cliché," she said. "However, it's necessary if we want private time."

Candace hadn't thought about it, but Lilian was just as famous as her husband. She'd been a Cover Girl for several years, and Candace could remember seeing her face on billboards when she was younger. The sports star and the model—now there was a cliché.

"How did you and John meet?" she asked.

"We met in junior high. We started dating in ninth grade when I was overweight and he couldn't throw a football if his life depended on it. Funny, huh?"

"Yeah," Candace said. "I guess you never can tell what someone will turn out to be."

"Well, we're both living proof that with hard work and dedication you can achieve your dreams. Sometimes life takes you on a strange route to get there. Look at John. When I met him, he didn't dream about being a football player; he dreamed about being Walt Disney. A lot of people thought that when he went after football, he was giving up on his dream. I knew better, though. He loves playing football. He loves playing anything, but ultimately it was all a means to achieving his dream."

"That's cool."

They walked into the mall and headed straight for a jewelry store. "I need an amethyst necklace," Lilian explained.

She found one she liked almost immediately. She then turned her attention to Candace. "What's your favorite stone?" she asked.

"I like emeralds," Candace admitted.

Lilian smiled. A minute later she had Candace trying on a gold cross pendant with an emerald in the center of it.

"What do you think?" she asked as Candace checked it out in the mirror.

"It's beautiful," Candace said.

"Great, we'll take this one too," Lilian told the saleswoman.

"But— "

"No buts, this was part of the terms of surrender."

"I was one of the ones surrendering, though. I'm not sure I should be partaking in the spoils of victory."

"It's a gift. I want you to have a memento of your Easter with us."

"Thank you."

"You're welcome."

After they left the jewelry store, they wandered through the mall. When they found the line to get pictures taken with the Easter Bunny, Lilian insisted that they get in it. A few minutes later Candace and Lilian were sitting beside the Easter Bunny having their picture taken. Lilian had taken off her scarf for the picture, and all around them people whipped out cell phones to take a picture.

"I have a feeling we're going to have to head home after this because we're not going to be able to get any more shopping done," Lilian said. "Sorry about that."

"No worries," Candace said as she smiled for the photo.

They purchased two copies. Lilian signed a few autographs, and then they beat a hasty retreat to her car. "Let's see what John is planning on cooking," Lilian said with a smile.

"Is he a good cook?" Candace asked.

"It depends entirely on what he's making," Lilian said. "His Mexican food is great. However, if he's planning on barbeque, choose the chicken. Trust me on this."

Back at the house they discovered that the kitchen was spotless, and the guys were in the back with the barbeque.

"Just in time," John said. "Candace, chicken or ribs?"

Candace glanced over at Lilian. "Chicken, definitely chicken."

Lilian smiled her approval.

"I love your mom," Candace told Josh later that night. "She's a lot of fun."

"I'm glad you two got along. I was a little worried," he confessed.

"Why?"

"Well, as you've pointed out, my family is definitely not normal. Not everyone can handle that. I was worried that you'd be here two hours and be ready to leave."

Candace shook her head. "I've having a wonderful time. To be honest, it's kind of refreshing. I'm also a bit jealous. I think you guys have more fun than anybody else."

Josh shrugged. "I think your family has a lot of fun too."

"Yeah, I guess it's just more conventional fun. By the way, my parents are totally serious about having all of you over to dinner in a couple of weeks."

"I think that will be awesome. There'll be enough of us we should totally play charades."

"Movie, TV show, book, or song," Candace said. "Charades is my parents' favorite party game."

"Speaking of movies, you want to head down to the theater?" Josh asked.

It sounded tempting, but she was tired. She also wanted to make sure she was rested for whatever was planned for the next day. "You know, I think I need to get some sleep," she said.

"Probably a good idea."

They said good night, and Candace retreated to her room. She closed the door and started laughing again at the décor. Lilian definitely had a wicked sense of humor.

She hung up some of her clothes in the closet and then got ready for bed. Before hopping in, she checked her phone and saw she had a text message from Tamara.

How is it going?

Candace smiled. She thought about calling but remembered that Tamara was at her grandmother's and three hours ahead, so she was probably already asleep.

She contented herself with sending a text message back. *Really good. Having fun.*

She set the phone down, but before she could get into bed it chirped. She flipped it open and saw the reply.

How much fun?

Candace sent her reply: *Too much. Food fight with the whole family. Shouldn't you be asleep?*

I wish. The bed's too hard.

Candace smiled. *Ouch! Talk to you later.*

She tossed the candy corn shaped pillows onto a chair, pulled back the covers, and crawled in. She was pleased to discover that she would not be having Tamara's problem. The bed was so comfortable she almost fell asleep before she reached to turn off the lamp on the nightstand.

The light clicked off, and Candace started laughing hysterically. The ceiling of the room was covered with glow-in-the-dark candy apple stickers.

17

Her phone rang at seven a.m., waking her up. "Hello?"

"I know it's early there, but I had to know what's going on," Tamara said.

Candace chuckled and filled her in.

"I'm jealous. You're having way more fun than me," Tamara lamented.

"If it's any consolation, James really misses you."

"That does make me feel a little bit better," Tamara admitted.

"Apparently he was thinking of trying to get an invitation to the reunion out of you."

"You mean he was willing to come spend Easter with my family?"

"Yes."

Tamara groaned in frustration. "I wish I had known that. I would totally have asked him, and we could be having a great time."

"Well, you know what they say: 'Absence makes the heart grow fonder.' "

"I don't want fonder. I want him here and kissing me."

"Sorry."

"Speaking of kissing. How are things with Josh?"

"We are just friends," Candace said, a little more forcefully than she had planned.

"Okay, backing off now," Tamara said.

They chatted for a couple more minutes, and then her phone indicated that her parents were trying to get hold of her. She hung up with Tamara, and her dad came on the line.

"Aunt Bess made it through the surgery just fine."

"Oh good."

"Yeah, the doctors even said she can come home tomorrow."

"That's a good Easter present," Candace said.

"We thought so. How are things going there?"

"Fine. John and Lilian are really nice."

"Oh, so it's John and Lilian, huh? Sounds like hobnobbing with celebrities is going to your head," he teased.

"Very funny, Dad."

"Hey, it turns out Aunt Bess lives less than an hour from Florida Coast."

"Really?" Candace asked.

"Yes, and she said you would be welcome there any time day or night," her dad added.

"Wow, I guess I won't be all alone," Candace said.

"Well, since Josh is going there too, I'm not sure you were ever going to be all alone."

"You know what I mean."

"Well, I should go. We love you."

"Love you too."

Candace got up, got dressed, and headed downstairs. A few minutes later everyone else joined her, and they had cereal, which to her relief, they didn't end up throwing at each other.

Once they had finished, Candace turned to Josh. "What's the game plan?"

He chuckled. "Very funny."

"I thought it was appropriate."

"Well, tonight we hold a vigil of sorts—prayer, meditation, that kind of thing."

"Wow."

"Yeah, it's pretty intense. Until then, though, the day is ours. So, what do you want to do?"

Candace smiled. "I heard that you had a pool."

That night Candace held a candle as she sat next to Josh in a pew in a small chapel. The chapel itself was about a five-minute drive from the house. There were a dozen other families present. A pastor led them in a few songs and then in prayer. After that he sat down with his own candle and left everyone to think and pray on their own.

It was a very moving experience. As Candace sat there she prayed for her family, especially her Aunt. She prayed for Lisa and her newfound faith. She prayed for Tamara and James and their relationship.

Next to her Josh stirred slightly. *God, watch over and guide Josh. Thank you for our friendship and all the ways that he has been there for me. He's an amazing guy. I pray that you give him strength and guidance.*

Suddenly her heart began to pound, and her hands started shaking slightly. She felt like she couldn't quite catch her breath. She wasn't sure what was wrong with her, but she felt dizzy and unbalanced. Just when she thought she was going to pass out, Josh took her hand in his.

Everything seemed to stop. She opened her eyes and stared down at his hand holding hers. Such a small gesture, but so powerful. There was so much strength in that hand and so much kindness as well.

She turned her head slightly so she could see his face. It was mere inches from hers. She studied his features in a way she never had before. As though feeling the weight of her stare, his eyes flickered open and he turned and looked at her.

He leaned forward, and his lips brushed hers for a moment. Then he dropped his head back down in prayer and closed his eyes. Candace forced her eyes away from him and stared instead into the heart of the candle she held.

God, what's happening? she asked.

On the way back to the house, everyone in the car was silent, still thinking and praying. Once home, they all headed upstairs. Candace lingered for a moment in her doorway, wanting desperately to talk to Josh but not sure what to say. He looked at her, smiled gently, and then disappeared into his own room.

She closed her door, walked over to the bed, and knelt down. She had a lot more praying to do before the morning.

In the morning they rose before sunrise and had prayer outside, which John led. Afterward they had brunch at the house. Extended family came, but Candace was too distracted to remember any of their names. Finally at two o'clock she found herself on the back lawn waiting for the start of the Easter-egg hunt.

Candace turned and saw Josh walking toward her, his jaw set and his stride purposeful. He had with him an array of objects that Candace was hard-pressed to identify.

"What is all that stuff?" she asked when he got close.

"Easter-egg-hunting gear. You know, night vision goggles, binoculars, metal detector, the usual."

"You have got to be kidding me!"

Josh smiled. "Nope. My family takes everything about Easter very seriously. When we say Easter-egg hunt, we mean *hunt*."

She wanted to talk about the kiss, but somehow it didn't seem appropriate for the time and place. She schooled herself to wait and focused instead on the game at hand.

"So, what does a girl have to do to get some equipment?"

"Well, I've got a catalog you can order some stuff from for next year," he teased.

"But I need it this year."

"Tell you what, I think I can spare this," he said, handing her the metal detector.

"Your generosity is overwhelming," she joked.

"I think so."

A minute later Lilian called them all together. "Okay, most of you know the rules. This year it was my job to hide the eggs. Eggs can be hidden anywhere on the grounds outside of the house. They may be made of plastic, paper, metal, candy, or be real eggs. Each egg has a point value assigned to it. The one with the most points is the winner. You will have one hour, which starts on my mark. Ready? Mark!"

Candace had never seen a group of people scatter in so many directions so quickly. She stood bewildered for a moment and then took off closer toward the house. Fewer people seemed to be headed in that direction, and as long as she was outside the house, she was in egg-hunting territory.

As she moved, she swept the ground with the metal detector and managed to discover three sprinkler heads and an earring. Up close to the house she continued to work the metal detector while scouring the bushes and plants with eyes and hands. When she had gone halfway around the house, she glanced at her watch and realized she only had fifteen minutes left. She picked up speed.

"Five minutes!" she heard Lilian shout through a bullhorn.

Candace started to jog, hoping at least to make it all the way around the perimeter. Suddenly, a flash of something purple caught her eye, and her metal detector went off at the same time.

Inside a potted plant, she discovered what looked like a Fabergé egg. She picked it up and ran back to the starting point, arriving with ten seconds to spare. Josh was right behind her, and she looked with disgust at the dozens of eggs of different sizes, shapes, and styles he had in a basket.

"Okay, time!" Lilian called. "Present eggs."

She went through tallying the points for the various eggs, most of which seemed to have their value printed or taped onto them. Candace inspected hers but didn't see a number. At last Lilian stopped in front of her.

"I just found one egg," Candace said, holding it up.

Lilian smiled. "You know the Bible parable about the pearl of great price?"

"Yes. The man who found it went out and sold all he had in order to obtain it."

"That's right. Open your egg."

Candace looked closer and saw the delicate catch. She flipped it, and the top of the egg swung open. Inside was a large, black pearl and a single sheet of paper.

"What does the paper say?" Lilian asked.

Candace opened it and read aloud, "Winner takes all."

She looked up at Lilian.

"Congratulations, you found the pearl, and you are the winner."

"What do I get?" Candace asked.

"You get to keep the pearl, say the blessing at dinner tonight, and be the one to hide eggs next year."

Candace started smiling and wasn't sure she would ever stop.

18

Candace sat on the edge of the stage with her fellow actors, head bowed in misery as Mr. Bailey paced in front of them. "That was, without a doubt, the worst final dress rehearsal I have ever seen," he said. Next to her, Keith groaned, and she reached out and patted him on the back. After all, it wasn't his fault he had thrown up on her.

"This is excellent news," Mr. Bailey continued.

"Excuse me?" Candace burst out before she could stop herself.

Mr. Bailey smiled at her. "In theater, the worse the final dress is, the better opening night is. I'm guessing that if tonight is any indication, tomorrow should be phenomenal."

"What if it's not?" Reed asked.

"Then expect to be pelted with rotten fruit," Mr. Bailey joked.

Candace glanced over at Tamara who looked like she was going to be ill. Tamara was the only one who hadn't messed up. She was probably worried about what the following night would bring for her.

"Go home, rest up. I'll see you here tomorrow at five o'clock."

Candace followed Tamara to her car and climbed wearily into the passenger seat.

"That could have gone a lot better," Candace sighed.

"At least you have nowhere to go but up," Tamara said, sounding worried.

"You'll be fine."

"I'm hungry. You wanna stop at Denny's?"

"Yes, please."

A few minutes later they ordered and sat back, sipping their sodas as they tried to relax. Suddenly Tamara stiffened.

"What is it?" Candace asked.

"I'm not sure you want to know," Tamara said.

"Well, now of course I do," Candace said. "What?"

Tamara nodded her head, and Candace turned to see Kurt and Lisa sharing a booth. The two were so deep in conversation that they didn't seem to have even noticed the food that was set before them. They were holding hands on the table.

Candace smiled. "Good for Lisa," she said.

"I'm still not down with the whole 'we-like-Lisa-now thing,'" Tamara said.

"She's had a hard life. It looks like she's taking more charge of it, though. I really think she and Kurt could be very happy together. I hope so at any rate."

"Very big of you."

Candace shrugged. "Kurt wasn't right for me. Doesn't mean I don't wish him happiness with someone he is right for."

"Does this mean you can finally move on ... as in, make a move on Josh?"

"Not talking about it," Candace said curtly. She and Josh still hadn't talked about the kiss they had shared in the chapel. She got the feeling that he was waiting for her to bring it up, but she hadn't been able to just yet. Until she talked about it with Josh, she didn't want to talk about it with anyone else, even Tamara.

"Fine, we can talk about something else, just not the play. I hope no one we know shows tomorrow night."

"I think I saw everyone we know, including every referee from The Zone out there," Tamara reported, coming backstage after having covertly scouted the auditorium. "That girl, Regina, who was in the Christmas play, was out there. Josh and James are of course here, and a bunch of your relatives and all of mine. Mom invited everybody," Tamara said, finishing with an eye roll.

Candace tried to keep her hands from shaking as she applied her makeup. She must have been out of her mind to invite people that she knew. Around her, the others were buzzing with excitement and nerves. Keith was sitting in a corner looking like he was going to throw up. Candace felt for him, but was too freaked out herself to try and encourage him. She had a feeling that if she tried to talk to him before the play, they'd both end up crying in the fetal position.

Tamara said she was nervous, but she didn't look like it. Her eyes were bright, she was bouncing around full of energy, and she was laughing at every joke people cracked.

Reed was sitting quietly, reading back over the script. Candace had thought about doing that, but then worried that she'd somehow mess herself up. She knew the lines; she had memorized them weeks ago. No need to panic herself about that needlessly.

Mr. Bailey had enough energy for ten men. It seemed like he was everywhere at once. He oversaw the makeup, he helped people warm up their voices, and he went over last-minute details with the prop people. She even spotted him brandishing Don Quixote's sword triumphantly over something.

"What's he doing?" Kira asked.

"Tilting at windmills," Candace joked.

"So, how are things with you and that hottie?" Kira asked.

"Good," Candace said, hesitating. "Complicated."

"I think you're making this harder than it really is," Kira said.

The last thing Candace wanted to do was discuss her love life with Kira. It did, however, keep her mind off the fact that she was going to be onstage in less than half an hour.

"I think I love him," Candace admitted.

"Awesome. I knew you two had chemistry."

"No, I mean, really love him," Candace said. "It's something more than a crush, stronger than liking or attraction. I love him, and I'm terrified of hurting him."

"Then don't."

It sounded so simple when Kira said it that way. Candace wanted to argue. It wasn't that simple; it was difficult and complicated. With the next breath, though, she wondered why that was. Josh hadn't done anything to make it complicated, neither had she. They were both available, and the attraction was clearly mutual. What was her problem?

"I think I'm scared that he's the one," Candace admitted, more to herself than Kira.

"Then he probably is," Kira said. "Look, I've got five older sisters. They dated a lot, but each one of them is married now. Every single one of them freaked out when they found the guy they were going to spend their life with. It was totally different. They were terrified because they knew it was life-changing, and people find change frightening."

Maybe that was it. It was weird in a way. She didn't know what the future held, but she did know that Josh was all the things she was discovering that she needed in a guy.

"Josh is funny and sweet and cute."

"Yes," Kira affirmed. "I could have told you that two seconds after meeting him."

"He also pushes me to do my best, makes me want to be a better person, and has been there every time I needed someone. He's taken care of me in ways I didn't even realize I needed to be taken care of until he showed me. He always goes out of his way to make sure that I'm happy."

"Sounds like you found one in a million," Kira said. "I'm jealous."

Candace smiled. "Thank you. I'm not sure I would have realized that without your help."

Kira shrugged. "You just needed a sounding board. If it hadn't been me, it would have been someone else—a friend, a classmate, a stranger in a grocery store."

Candace laughed and turned new eyes on Kira. "How come we're not friends?" she asked.

"Because, as we've already established, you're an idiot," Kira said with a grin.

Candace reached out and hugged her. "Thank you for pointing that out."

"Any time."

"So, what's your story?" Candace asked as they broke away.

Kira grinned. "Still looking for Mr. Right."

"Keep looking," Candace said.

"You know it. These days a girl just can't sit still and wait for her guy to find her."

"What are we talking about?" Tamara asked, pulling up a chair.

"Boys, naturally," Kira said.

"I'm in love with Josh," Candace admitted, blushing as she did so.

"I'm glad you finally figured that out," Tamara said.

"You knew?"

"Of course I knew. James knows. Your parents know. Anyone who knows you and has half a brain knows."

"Well, how come no one ever told me?"

"Because it would have ruined the surprise," Tamara said with a smile.

Candace smiled back. "What a nice surprise it turned out to be."

"All right, people, gather around," Mr. Bailey said, standing in the middle of the room.

Everyone pulled up a chair and sat down.

"Okay, people. Tonight is the night all your hard work pays off. I'm proud of all of you. I've never seen a group work harder. You're going to be great. Just relax and have fun. We've got a full house out there so enjoy it and break a leg!"

Candace joined in the round of applause. Her butterflies came back in full force. Keith looked a little better than he had a few minutes before. Maybe they would all make it through in one piece. Candace hoped so. She did know, though, that whatever happened it wouldn't change the fact that she was in love with a wonderful guy.

"Okay, we go on in five. Everyone take your places," Mr. Bailey said.

"Moment of truth," Tamara said, jumping to her feet.

"I wish I could be as calm about it as you are," Candace said.

"Calm, are you kidding? My mom threatened to call a vet and get a horse tranquilizer before I left the house."

Candace laughed. "So, you're saying all the energy is because you're totally neurotic?"

"Exactly. I haven't been able to remember a single one of my lines for the last two hours," Tamara admitted.

Candace stared at her. "What are you going to do?"

"No clue. That's okay, though. I'm hoping that if I choke, someone else can think of something."

"Don't look at me," Kira said. "I started grilling Candace about her love life just so I wouldn't have to go to the bathroom and throw up ... again."

Candace stared from one to the other. "You two are unbelievable. Both of you seem to have it totally together, and now I find out that I'm actually the mellow one in this group?"

"Can you spell irony?" Kira asked.

"I get it," Candace said.

"No, seriously, can you spell it? I just realized I'm so paralyzed with fear I'm losing basic cognitive abilities."

Candace turned to Tamara. "Call your mom and tell her we need two horse tranquilizers."

"She invited everyone she could to this thing, including our family doctor. It's possible he has a valium sample on him," Tamara joked.

"Let's go find him and ask," Kira said.

"Thanks, you two, you've really helped me out," Candace said.

"Yeah, how?" Tamara asked.

"I realized that I'm in great shape compared to everyone else here."

"Lucky you," Keith groaned as he walked by her.

"All right, let's get where we have to go," Candace said.

They scattered. When Candace made it to her spot, she found Mr. Bailey waiting for her.

"Any final direction?" she asked.

"Candace, the stage is yours. Remember that. It doesn't belong to the audience, it belongs to you. Take them by the hand and tell them the story you want to tell them. Don't let them dictate the story to you. Can you do that?"

"I'm not sure, but I hope so," she admitted.

"Acting is life; life is acting. All the world's a stage, and we just play our parts. I really believe that. It's up to everyone to understand the part they're playing and to communicate it effectively to friends, family, strangers, and even enemies. Do you understand?"

"Are you telling me that I have to make my own choices, not let others choose for me?"

"Exactly, because ultimately it is up to you how your life plays out. The audience can try to bully you into thinking they're right, but they're not. God is the ultimate theater critic. Just like any theater critic, he will judge you, the actor, on the choices you make. He won't blame or praise the audience on your behalf."

"Wow. That's profound."

"That's life. That's theater. Fate may be the playwright who sets events in motion and peoples your life with characters. It is entirely up to you to provide the deeper meaning, the subtext."

"But what if I don't like the play?"

"Then you have the power to change it. The words are just words. They're empty without the emotion behind them. Most circumstances can be comedic, just as most can be tragic. A great actor can make *Romeo and Juliet* a farce and mold *Much Ado About Nothing* into a tragedy."

"I'm not that great an actor," Candace said.

"No, you're not. However, you are that great a person. Make your life what you want of it, and don't be afraid to find your own meaning. In your life you should be the star, not the supporting actress."

He walked away, and a moment later the curtain went up. Tamara messed up her first line but then recovered and went on to perform brilliantly. Keith pulled it together right before he went on stage, and Candace had never heard him sing so powerfully or mournfully as then.

Candace threw herself wholeheartedly into the story and tried to live it moment by moment, not anticipating the future, but living the present reality for the character. She felt like she brought Aldonza's story to life, and somehow it was also her story.

When the final curtain fell, she was trembling from exhaustion and had sweated away half her makeup, but she felt completely alive. The curtains rose again for people to take their bows. The cheers of the crowd were deafening as they echoed throughout the auditorium.

Candace watched as Tamara and two others took their bows. James and Tamara's father came forward out of the audience and each handed Tamara a bouquet of roses.

When it was finally her turn, Candace ran out onto the stage and took a bow. Keith handed her a bouquet of flowers, and she bowed again. On the floor a couple of people had approached the foot of the stage. Her father, Josh, Gib, and Pete all handed her flowers as well.

Her arms full, she stepped back and let Keith stride to center stage. He bowed and then motioned for the rest of the cast to join him. They linked hands as best they could and bowed as one. Then Keith pointed toward Mr. Bailey in the front row, and he stood up and took a bow.

Candace looked out and saw that the crowd was on its feet. She felt the excitement of the moment washing over her. She was living her life in the limelight, and for the first time she realized that she didn't want it any other way.

19

Candace woke up the next morning with butterflies in her stomach. *Showtime*, she thought to herself as she got out of bed. She had made it through the school play, now it was time to take on Talent Show.

I can do this, she told herself. *Just relax and breathe.* She got dressed in black jeans and a black T-shirt. She braided her hair so that it would be back and out of her way. She had several hours to kill, but she had already decided to spend them in the park.

When she got to The Zone, she could tell by the number of cars in the referee parking lot that she wasn't the only one with that idea. She parked and entered the park, walking slowly, taking in the sights and sounds. She came across the train just as it was pulling into the station, and Pete motioned to her.

"What's up?" she asked after walking over.

He opened the door to the engine. "Hop up," he said.

"Really?" She didn't think Pete ever let anyone ride in the engine.

"Yup."

He lent her a hand as she climbed in and then motioned to the other seat. She sat down gently, staring around with interest. A minute later they were pulling out of the station.

"How are you doing?" he asked.

"Nervous," she admitted.

"Me too."

"I like it up here," she said after a minute. "I can see why you love this job."

"Yeah, I wouldn't change it for any in the world. Candace, I wanted to thank you."

"For what?"

"For making me one of your groupies," he said wryly.

"Groupie?"

"Yeah. I'm not sure you realize just how popular you are here. Everyone loves you. You've helped a lot of us out too. I appreciate the fact that I actually had a team that chose me for Talent Show this year. Every year I'm usually the last pick for any of the big activities, and people are unhappy to have me at that."

"I was freaked out when I found out you were on my scavenger hunt team over the summer," she admitted.

"I know, but that didn't stop you from being nice. I appreciate being included."

"I'm glad, but things like that are going to make it that much harder to leave."

"Don't worry about me. I'm going to be fine, better than fine. Besides, I figure Sue and I can keep each other out of trouble while you're off in Florida."

"I'll have to check in on you two on my breaks, though."

"You better, or else," he said.

"Else what?"

"I'll start trying to run you over again."

She threw back her head and laughed.

A couple hours later she was standing in the crowd watching as team after team demonstrated their talent. Her group was slated as one of the last. Waiting was just making her more nervous.

"And now put your hands together for the Kowabunga Krew!"

Candace clapped and shouted. Josh, Mark, and the others ran up onto the stage with instruments and surfboards. Within seconds they were set up. The musicians set up on the left of the stage. On the right a couple of guys jumped on surfboards and were hoisted into the air by their comrades. The guitarist played an opening chord, and then they began to sing Surfin' Safari with Josh singing the lead.

Candace screamed and cheered. The guys holding the surfboards lifted them up and down and teetered them so it looked like the guys riding them were actually surfing. It was awesome-looking. They sounded great too.

At the end of the song, the two surfers tumbled off their boards in a simulated wipeout. The Krew took their bows and then hustled offstage to make room for the next group.

Up next was one of the teams who worked in the Kids Zone. After them, it would be their turn, so Candace made her way to the side of the stage where the rest of her team had already gathered.

She arrived just in time to see Corinne freak out.

"I don't think we should do Stonehenge. I can't remember it!" Corinne said, her voice panicked. "Can't we make a model of one of the rides? What about the Sky Tower?"

Pete grabbed her by the shoulders and shook her. "Pull yourself together, woman, that's at Sea World!"

"We're going to do Stonehenge. There's no turning back now," Traci said. "No matter how scared you are." She glanced at Candace.

Candace nodded encouragingly. "We can do this. We've practiced for it, and we're ready."

"We're all in this together," Sue added.

Candace had no clue what the team on the stage was doing. She just focused on her teammates and picked up her set of cups. "We know we're better than the Kowabunga Krew," she said. "They were good. We're better. That's all we need."

There was a round of applause. The moment of truth. Candace took a deep breath.

"Thank you. And now ... Candy and the Apples!"

Candace jerked. "Okay, who do I kill?" she asked her team.

Sue burst out laughing, and then so did everyone else, including Corinne. The tension eased, and they turned and ran onto the stage. They took their places to start with Stonehenge. In the middle of the stage, Pete knelt down and began to pound out a rhythm with the cups. Then methodically and to the rhythm, the other four began to build Stonehenge. When Candace and Sue finished their parts, they took over drumming out the beat while Pete built the center and Corinne and Traci finished their parts. When they were done, people cheered. They stood for a moment, then they took down the structures at twice the speed they put them up.

They paused, then started on the Eiffel Tower, moving much faster than they had on Stonehenge. It went up smoothly, and when it was finished they all stood and moved back for a moment. The crowd cheered. They moved back in and took it down even faster, splitting the cups between them.

Then they took their places for the three pyramids. Pete started it off by beating the rhythm impossibly fast. On the fifth beat, they all began, putting the pyramids up lightning fast to cheers and whistles from the crowd. They finished simultaneously, took a step back, then a step forward and slammed it all down into the ground in five stacks.

They stood up and bowed as the crowd went wild. "We did it!" Corinne gasped. "I don't believe it."

"We rock," Candace confirmed.

They took a final bow then grabbed their cups and ran off the stage. Next to the stage Candace ran into Becca who grabbed her arm. Candace looked at her friend and saw fear in her eyes.

"What's wrong?" Candace asked.

"I need sugar."

"Excuse me?"

"For the dance. I can't do that dance without sugar. I had some stashed so I could eat it right before we go on, but someone's found it and taken it. I went to my backup stash and it was gone too. All the carts are empty and locked. What am I going to do?"

"Hold tight," Candace said, turning and pushing through the crowd as fast as she could. She finally broke into the clear and ran toward the Candy Counter. She made it inside and snatched up a candy apple then turned and raced back.

"And now, the Muffin Mansion presents *The Lady of the Dance*!"

"I need sugar!" she heard Becca shriek as she got close to the stage.

She saw someone with a pack of gum, and another person with a candy bar try to give them to Becca only to be blocked by people in the crowd.

Becca was standing in the middle of the stage, a look of terror on her face. The rest of the Muffin Mansion team was in line behind her, ready to begin. The music started. The rest of the dancers began their routine. Candace tried to push through the crowd, but her way was blocked.

"Becca!" Candace shouted, trying to get her attention.

Becca turned and saw Candace. Candace cocked back her arm and threw the candy apple as hard as she could. It flipped end over end as it sailed through the air. Several in the crowd jumped up in an attempt to intercept it, but it was beyond their reach.

Becca reached up and snatched it out of the air. There was a long pause and then she brought it to her mouth and bit into it. Candace held her breath. Becca closed her eyes for a moment. Suddenly they flew back open and she tossed the candy apple into the crowd. Her feet began to move unbelievably fast and then she was off, dancing and jumping and spinning out of control.

When Becca spun into her final pose and the dance ended, the crowd erupted. At that moment Candace knew her team had lost, and yet, she couldn't have been happier.

It turned out they were the last group to go. After two minutes John Hanson got up on the stage and took the microphone.

"Wow, I think we can all agree that everyone here outdid themselves. That was amazing, and you all should be very proud. Give yourselves a hand!"

Everyone applauded, and it lasted for nearly a minute. Finally it died down and he continued. "We have the winners of the contest. Anyone interested in hearing?"

There were cheers and shouts.

"Okay. Here goes. In third place we have the Kowabunga Krew!"

Josh and his team cheered as they ran up on stage to accept their trophy.

Candace clenched her fists. They had been great, but she knew her team was better. She just hoped the judges had agreed.

"In second place we have ... Candy and the Apples!"

Candace and Sue started screaming and jumping up and down as they tried to make their way to the stage. Finally they got up on it and were joined by the rest of their team. Pete handed Candace the trophy, and she hoisted it high in the air. She found Josh in the crowd and did a little victory dance. He just shook his head and grinned.

They ran back down into the crowd.

"And now for our winners. Once again, congratulations to everyone. We all won because of the quality of the performances. I can't remember a Talent Show I've enjoyed more than this one," John said. "The winners are ... the Muffin Mansion!"

Candace screamed and jumped up and down as Becca and the rest of the gang claimed their trophy.

"Congratulations to the Muffin Mansion, and thank you all for that stirring rendition of *The Lady of the Dance*!" John said.

The crowd roared its approval. The group accepted their trophy, waved to the crowd, did a five-step routine, and then ran back offstage.

"Congratulations!" Candace told Becca as she showed her the trophy.

Once the noise died down a bit, John continued. "Now, I'd like to take this opportunity to congratulate all the scholarship candidates. You've all done outstanding work here, and I have every confidence in your abilities. I hope to see you all working for The Zone for a long, long time."

Candace's heart was pounding in her chest, and she had a hard time catching her breath. She had tried to fixate on the talent portion of the show and put this out of her mind. Now it was here, the moment of truth. She squeezed Becca's hand so hard that the other girl began to squirm.

"Ouch!"

Candace tried to loosen her grip and then gave up.

"This year's winner of The Zone scholarship to Florida Coast is Candace Thompson!"

"You won!" Roger shouted, crushing her and Becca in a hug.

"Candace, come on up here!" John shouted.

She let go of Roger and Becca and moved toward the stage in a daze. Suddenly there was music playing, and she began to laugh hysterically when she recognized it as "I Want Candy."

She walked up onto the stage and shook John's hand. He winked at her, and she grinned back. It was so weird to see him in public now that she had spent time at his home.

"You earned it," he said. "I can't wait to ride Balloon Races."

"Me either," she said.

She accepted a certificate from him, and then he handed her the microphone.

She looked out at the sea of faces and was able to pick out several. She smiled at everyone.

"Thank you. I wouldn't be standing up here if it weren't for the help and support and encouragement of everyone here. I know some of you really well and others not nearly as well as I'd like, but you have all made a huge impact on my life.

"When I started here last summer as a cotton candy operator, it was just a job ... and I wasn't sure I wanted one in the first place. Things were hard, but I made it through with the help of so many of you. And somewhere along the way I began to feel like I belonged somewhere.

"I've never known what I wanted to do with my life, but it has become clear to me that my heart, my future, is with The Zone. I'm going away for a while, but I'll be back. And when I am, we're going to build some awesome rides!"

A cheer went up from the crowd. It wasn't nearly the kind of inspirational speech John gave on a routine basis, but it was from her heart. She handed him back the microphone and then made her way off the stage to rejoin her friends. Tears filled her eyes, but she didn't care. She was going to miss everyone when she went to Florida, but she'd be back.

Sue hugged her as she walked past, and Candace clung to her fiercely for a moment before continuing on. Lisa grabbed her next. Of all her friends at The Zone, Lisa was the most surprising. Candace was still shocked at how their relationship had changed. They hugged for a moment, and then Candace continued on. Traci and Corinne both hugged her. All the cart vendors and the refs from the Candy Counter clustered around to congratulate her and pat her back.

Martha smiled, and Candace could see that she was crying. Pete kissed her on the cheek and thrust a small toy train into her hand. The crew of the Muffin Mansion surrounded her. Becca, Gib, and Roger embraced her together. Over the top of Becca's head she could see Kurt. He smiled at her and she smiled back.

Then finally she saw Josh. He smiled at her in that same laid-back way he had the first time she met him, and her heart leaped. She ran toward him, and he wrapped her in his arms, kissing her like she'd never been kissed before. She pulled away slightly. "We need to talk," she said.

He grinned. "Actually I think we've done too much talking and not enough of this." He had a point, and she smiled as she kissed him again. Of all the gifts The Zone had given her, he was by far the best.

The night of Tamara's party arrived, and Candace and her parents showed up at Boone's. Candace shivered with excitement as they were led up winding stairs to the top of the Fort. The restaurant itself was a juxtaposition of the rustic and the refined. The tables and chairs looked like rough-hewn wood and were slightly twisted to follow the curve of the wood. The tables were set with the finest linen, china, crystal, and silver.

"Bizarre. I like it," her mom said.

Josh walked toward them. "Welcome to Boone's," he said.

"Aren't you a little afraid of exposing your secret tonight?" her father asked by way of greeting.

Josh shrugged. "I eat dinner here with my parents a lot. The staff here is already in the know."

"Looks like your parents just arrived," her mom said.

"Great, let me introduce you," he said, waving to them.

John and Lilian came over. Lilian embraced Candace. "I've missed you," she said.

"I've missed you too," Candace replied.

"Mom, Dad, I'd like you to meet Candace's parents, Mr. and Mrs. Thompson. Mr. and Mrs. Thompson, these are my parents, John and Lilian."

"Call us Rob and Carol," her father said as they all shook hands.

"It's so nice to meet the parents of the girl who has completely bewitched my youngest son," John said with a smile.

Josh actually blushed. It made Candace smile.

"We're just thrilled that she and Josh are finally dating," Carol said.

It was Candace's turn to blush, and Josh laughed.

"I hear there's a game night in the works," Lilian said.

"Absolutely, we'd love to have you over next Friday if that works for you," Rob said.

"Sounds great," Lilian said.

More people came upstairs, and Candace and her parents took their seats as John and Lilian moved to greet them.

"I like them," Rob said.

"They seem lovely," Carol added.

"I'm glad," Candace said as she looked around, wondering where Josh went.

He returned a minute later with a wicked grin on his face. He was holding something behind his back.

"What have you got there?" she asked.

"I just thought you'd like to see a sneak peek of something that showed up today."

"What?"

"It's a mock-up of the cover for The Zone yearbook."

Candace groaned. "I still can't believe no one but you told me we had a yearbook."

"Spend more time on the website."

"Why should I when I have my own personal insider who's supposed to tell me things?"

"Fair enough," he said with a laugh.

"Okay, show me the cover."

He handed it to her. There on the cover, spelled out in different types of candies were the words I Want Candy.

She started laughing so hard she nearly fell out of her chair. "You have got to be kidding me!"

"Nope. You want to hear the best part?"

"Yes."

"I had nothing to do with it."

"That is good," she said.

She passed the cover to her parents who also started laughing.

"Yup, we pass those out just before summer starts," he said.

"You know what's weird?" Candace said.

"What?"

"It's nearly the end of spring, we'll be going to Florida in September, and there isn't any other job you're trying to entice me to come back for."

"Ah, the perks and drawbacks of being a regular employee," he said.

"It's just a little weird that I'll have this job until I go away to school."

"You know, I was thinking about that. Zone World has a summer international cultural exchange program where you get to work and live with college students from all over the world."

"That could be a lot of fun," she said. "But why are you telling me this?"

"Well, I just figured you might want to consider enrolling in it. You could get a roommate from Italy or Japan or China."

"And?"

"And you could work in the Asia Marketplace selling rice candy."

She blinked at him for a moment. "Are you serious?"

"Dead serious."

She sighed and rolled her eyes. "I'm sorry, but I don't see a summer of rice candy in my future."

"Never say never," he said as he leaned in to kiss her.

Discussion Questions

for *The Spring of Candy Apples*

- Candace finally realizes she needs to break it off with Kurt. What clues did she have that Kurt wasn't the one for her? Was she paying attention, or trying to avoid the clues? Would you have broken it off sooner, or stayed in the relationship in the hope that it would get better?

- As best friends, it seems natural that Tamara and Candace would want to attend the same college and room together. What are the advantages and disadvantages to this? Would you want to go to a school with good friends (or even just people you knew), or would you opt to go someplace entirely new and without connections?

- In the class play, Don Quixote has faith in Aldonza, encouraging her to become the woman he believes she can be. Who are the people in your life who do this for you? (Your parents? A brother or sister? Friend? Boyfriend?) How does your belief in *their* faith in you bless *them* in return?

- Becca tells Candace very simply that "Kurt wasn't a keeper ... because (they) want very different things out of life" (72). For instance, Candace and Kurt never talked about the fact that Candice was a Christian and Kurt wasn't. Would you be willing to date someone fully knowing you didn't share the same faith? Would you bring it up? When? Is this even negotiable?

- Candace is able to design a theme park ride for the scholarship competition. If you could design any ride you wanted, what would it be?

- Candace has never enjoyed being in the spotlight. She even puts up a fuss when, two weeks before their class play, Josh insists that they'll be in attendance for sure. Is Candace simply humble? Or does she have a lack of self-confidence?

- Lisa despised Candace because of all the things Candace had that she didn't. She loathed Candace because her life had crumpled, and Candace's had gotten fame. Have you ever felt the same way toward others: they had something you wanted, and jealousy kept you from befriending or getting to know them?

- "Acting is life; life is acting. All the world's a stage, and we just play our parts" (173). This quote directly supports Candace's struggle to gain confidence in the series. She is an actor on her own stage. In theory, this concept is very encouraging. But how about the backstage people who highlight the main actors? Which would you rather be? Which do you think you are?

- At what point did you know that Josh and Candace would end up as a couple?

- The last lines of the book suggest that maybe Candace will do the cultural exchange program—and take on the job selling rice candy. What do you think? Would you do the exchange?

New York Times Bestselling Author

DEBBIE VIGUIÉ

the summer of cotton candy

Read chapter 1 of The *Summer of Cotton Candy*, Book 1 in Sweet Seasons.

1

Candace Thompson wondered where her life had gone wrong. Maybe when she was fourteen, she should have babysat her bratty cousin when her parents asked. Maybe when she was seven, if she hadn't locked the teacher out of the classroom, this wouldn't be happening to her. No, maybe her life went all wrong when she was three and she knocked down the girl with the pigtails who had stolen Mr. Huggles, her stuffed bear. Yes, the more she thought about it, that must have been the moment that started her on the path that led to the special punishment she was now suffering.

It was the first day of summer vacation, but for Candace, it might as well have been the last. She sat in a dark dreary office, signing away her freedom. The decree had come down from her father: she had to get a job. No job, no cash. No cash, no movies or hanging with her friends. It didn't matter to him that if she had a job she wouldn't have time to do the things she would need the money for.

She took a deep breath as she finished filling out the last form and handed it across the desk to the recruiter, Lloyd Peterson, a strange-looking man in a frumpy brown suit whom she was convinced had to be a perv. Hadn't she seen him on

America's Most Wanted? She slid down into her seat, willing herself to be invisible, or at least small enough to slip away unnoticed.

"Candace," he mused, "can I call you Candy?"

"Well ..." She was about to say no. She hated that name.

"Great. So, Candy, what makes you want to work for The Zone?"

She didn't want to work for The Zone, she just wanted to enjoy her summer like everybody else. Her father had put his foot down, though. According to him it was time she learned the value of work and earning her own way. She had chosen to work for The Zone because she had absolutely no skills, and working for a theme park seemed more interesting than flipping burgers.

She sighed and squirmed, refusing to meet the recruiter's eyes. "I've always dreamed of working for The Zone. I want to be part of the excitement and help people enjoy themselves more." It was her rehearsed answer, and she held her breath, hoping he would buy it.

He stared at her for a long minute before nodding. Picking up a bright blue folder on his desk, he flipped it open and cleared his throat. "You realize, of course, that if you wanted a summer job, you should have started applying months ago, right?" he asked, staring at her over the tops of his glasses.

She slunk farther down into her chair. She licked her lips when she realized he expected an answer. "No," she said.

"No? No? Well, you are wrong. In order to get a good summer job, you should start applying at least in March."

March! All I could think of in March was holding out until spring break without going postal. Her eyes were now nearly level with the edge of his desk. "I just thought, you know, The Zone needs a lot of employees."

"You are correct, but most of our summer positions have already been filled."

He stopped and stared at her. She wasn't sure what he expected her to say, but she was beginning to have the sinking feeling that her summer would consist of asking people if they wanted fries with their meal.

Just as she was about to get up to leave, sure that the interview had come to an end, he spoke. "We do, however, have two openings."

She sat up. "What are they?"

"The first is janitorial."

"You mean those people who go around sweeping up after everyone?" *That might not be so bad. At least I could keep moving, and nobody ever pays attention to them.*

He raised an eyebrow. "Some of our janitorial employees do that, but not this position. This one is cleaning up the women's restrooms."

Candace's stomach turned. In her mind she pictured the high-school bathroom by fourth period, and that was only with a few hundred users, not thousands. There was no way she was going there.

"Um, and the other one is ...?" she managed to ask as diplomatically as she could.

"Cotton candy operator."

"I'll take it!" she exclaimed, more loudly than she had meant to.

"Good!" Lloyd stood up and opened a drawer in one of his many filing cabinets. He pulled out a stack of papers two inches thick and slammed them down on his desk right in front of her. The desk continued to shake for a moment as though there had just been an earthquake. "Fill those out."

"Now?" she asked, her mind boggling over the enormity of the task. She moved slightly so that she was eye level with the stack, and she could feel her hand begin to cramp up in premature protest.

"Yes, now. You can, however, use the table in the courtyard if you'd be more comfortable."

The word *duh* came to mind, but she bit her tongue and kept it to herself.

"Yes, sir, thank you. I'll do that," she said instead, scrambling to her feet and grabbing the stack of papers. She made her way out of the room as fast as she could, taking a deep breath once in the hallway.

The hallways around this place are roomier than the offices, she thought to herself as she immediately began to feel less claustrophobic. She turned around, not sure which way the courtyard would be. She hadn't seen one on her way in, so it must be in the other direction.

She came to a T in the hall and craned her neck to the right. All she could see that way were more offices, so she turned to the left ...

... and ran straight into a six-foot wall.

"Umph," the wall gasped as Candace's papers went flying in all directions.

"I am so sorry," Candace said, realizing that the wall she had run into was actually a guy, a *big* guy, a guy with muscles she could see through his shirt. She looked up and forgot what she was going to say next. She was staring at the Lone Ranger. He stood there, larger than life in pale blue, complete with boots and gun belt. Black wavy hair shone from underneath a white hat pushed far back on his head. A black mask covered part of his face.

All this was not what stopped her in her tracks, though. What took her breath away and caused her to stare like an idiot were his eyes. He had amazing eyes that were bright blue and crackled like lightning. He stared right through her, and her heart began to hammer.

"I—I—"

He smiled at her, and she felt dizzy. "Are you lost, my lady?"

She nodded, still unable to look away from those piercing eyes.

"Here, let me help you," he said, bending down.

For one dizzying moment his face came close to hers, and she thought he was going to kiss her just like in some movie.

Instead of kissing her, though, he knelt down and began picking up her papers.

Idiot, she said to herself, feeling her cheeks burning. Her knees began to buckle, and she covered it by quickly dropping down to her knees and scooping up some of the papers that had managed to spread themselves across the width of the hall.

"I'm such a klutz," she said.

"Not at all. How could you expect to run into something when you're not looking where you're going?"

She glanced up quickly, stunned at the rebuke. Then she noticed that he was grinning from ear to ear. They both burst out laughing.

"That should do it," he said finally, handing her the last sheet of paper. His fingers brushed hers, and she felt her stomach do a flip-flop.

"Thanks."

"So, where are you headed?"

"Um, um," she stammered for a moment, her mind going completely blank.

"I take it you're filling these out?" he said, tapping the stack of papers.

She nodded, relieved as she remembered, "Something was said about a courtyard that had a table."

"I'll show you where it is."

She fell into step with him, and he led her down the corridor. They made three quick turns in a row and arrived at a door leading out to what truly was a small courtyard.

"There you go," he said, holding the door open for her. She walked outside into the sun and plunked her papers down onto a table.

"Thanks."

"I live to serve."

She couldn't think of something witty to say, so she just stared at him.

He winked at her. "I'll see you around."

Then he turned and left. She sank down into the chair, her knees feeling weak. "Who was that masked man?"

Four hours and three phone calls to her father later, Candace finished filling out the application. She stacked up the tax forms, identity forms, nondisclosure forms, noncompetition agreements, and receipt-of-employee-handbook forms. And with a snort, she put the background check and financial disclosure form on top of the whole stack. She was seventeen, and she had no finances to disclose. She'd had a momentary panic about the background check until she realized they were looking for things like a criminal background or drug use and wouldn't be interested in the fact that she'd had detention twice in seventh grade.

She flipped back through the employee handbook. It was over a hundred pages long. After reading through it, she realized that The Zone had a policy and procedure for absolutely everything. They even had three different emergency-evacuation plans, depending on whether it was fire, weapons problems, or natural disasters. Clearly the people who worked on the handbook were paranoid, and now, after reading it, so was she.

She dragged herself to her feet, her stomach angrily reminding her that lunch had been hours before and she had missed it. She miraculously made her way back through the maze of corridors to Mr. Peterson's office. He was speaking on the phone, so she stood in the doorway until he looked up and saw her.

He hung up the phone. "Come in, Candy. I take it you're done?"

She nodded, handing him the stack.

"Excellent. Well, I'll take a look at all these. I'm sure they're in order. Let me just get copies of your driver's license and social security card."

She fished them out of her purse and handed them to him. He left the office for a minute and then returned with photocopies. He handed her cards back to her.

"Okay, you'll start orientation tomorrow."

"Tomorrow?" she asked.

"Yes, is there a problem with that?" he asked sharply.

"I just thought I'd have a couple of days before — "

"Tomorrow's our last orientation class for the summer. It's either tomorrow or never."

Never *wasn't* an option, no matter how much she wanted it to be. A vision of a certain masked man flitted briefly through her mind. Then again, maybe this wasn't going to be so bad after all.

"Tomorrow. Tomorrow is fine for me," she said.

"Report to the lobby at seven forty a.m."

There went any hope she had of sleeping in, probably forever. She sighed and nodded.

"What do you mean you have to be home early tonight?" Candace's best friend, Tamara Wilcox, huffed over the phone. "I thought we were hanging out?"

"We can still hang. I just need to get some sleep. I have to start work early in the morning," Candace explained. She flipped onto her back and braced her legs against the wall next to her bed.

There was only silence on the other end of the phone.

"Tam, you still there?"

"Uh-huh. Meet me at Starbucks."

"Can't. I'm getting a job to earn summer spending money, and Dad won't give me an advance."

"I'm buying. Just get your butt over here."

Ten minutes later Candace was sitting down at a corner table where Tamara was already waiting for her. Without a word, Tamara slid a grande hot chocolate with a shot of raspberry across the table to her.

Candace blew through the tiny opening in the lid like she always did. Tonight, though, the whistling sound it produced didn't make her smile. She was too busy trying to avoid looking at the daggers in Tamara's eyes.

"So, you're ditching me for the summer?"

"No, just five days a week. I should be free evenings and weekends."

"Did they guarantee that?"

"Well, no, but they said it would likely be that. They couldn't expect me to work during church, you know?"

Tamara crossed her arms over her chest, a sure sign she wasn't buying it. "And what about youth group? Even if they don't make you work Sunday morning they're going to make you work Friday nights."

"I should be free evenings," Candace said, slinking down into her seat and hating that she was repeating herself. Somehow, it sounded less plausible than it had earlier in the recruiter's office.

"And if you're not? It's bad enough you're going to be blowing off church and youth group, but what about me? I'm your best friend. What kind of summer am I going to have without you?"

"Come on, no matter what hours I get, it will only be thirty-five a week. We can still do all kinds of stuff. And I'll have the money to pay for it," Candace said with a sigh. It was amazing sometimes how Tamara could turn anyone's pain into her own.

Tamara uncrossed her arms and leaned forward, tapping one perfectly manicured nail on the table. "You know, if money is the issue, I can take care of that."

Candace stared at her. Tamara was rich. Her whole family was. Her monthly allowance was more than some people made in a year. Candace knew she was serious, and it was a tempting offer.

"I can't," she said at last, tears of frustration filling her eyes. "My dad would kill me."

Tamara sat back, a disappointed look on her face. "Oh, is he pulling that rite-of-passage, learn-the-value-of-work crap on you?"

Candace nodded and wiped her eyes with the back of her hand. "Yeah, he'd freak if I backed out. And I don't think you're prepared to pay for my college tuition."

Tamara laughed. "Would it get you to bail on this whole Zone thing?"

Candace scowled. "He's my dad. What can I do?"

"Nothing," Tamara said, shaking her head. "Parents are so much work."

Sweet Seasons by Debbie Viguié!

Join Candace Thompson on a sweet, lighthearted, and honest romp through the friendships, romances, family and friend dramas, and faith discoveries that make a girl's life as full as it can be.

Summer of Cotton Candy

Softcover: 978-0-310-71558-0

Fall of Candy Corn

Softcover: 978-0-310-71559-7

Winter of Candy Canes

Softcover: 978-0-310-71752-2

Spring of Candy Apples

Softcover: 978-0-310-71753-9

Also available in ebook versions.

Available in stores and online!

Visit www.zondervan.com/teen

Real Life Series from Nancy Rue

Four girls are brought together through the power of a mysterious book that helps them sort through the issues of their very real lives.

Motorcycles, Sushi and One Strange Book

Softcover: 978-0-310-71484-2

Boyfriends, Burritos and an Ocean of Trouble

Softcover: 978-0-310-71485-9

Tournaments, Cocoa and One Wrong Move

Softcover: 978-0-310-71486-6

Limos, Lattes & My Life on the Fringe

Softcover: 978-0-310-71487-3

Also available in ebook and enhanced ebook versions.

Available in stores and online!

Talk It Up!

Want free books?
First looks at the best new fiction?
Awesome exclusive merchandise?

We want to hear from you!

Give us your opinions on titles, covers, and stories. Join the Z Street Team.

Email us at zstreetteam@zondervan.com to sign up today!

Also—Friend us on Facebook!

www.facebook.com/goodteenreads

- Video Trailers
- Connect with your favorite authors
- Sneak peeks at new releases
- Giveaways
- Fun discussions
- And much more!

CPSIA information can be obtained
at www.ICGtesting.com
Printed in the USA
BVHW082350211120
593554BV00009B/181

9 780310 717539